Our Little Wedding

S.L. STERLING

OUR LITTLE WEDDING

by

S.L. STERLING

© 2023

Ainsley

"Anyone want coffee?" I questioned.

I stood in front of the sink, washing the last of the dinner dishes.

"Love some," my father called out.

"Yes, please," Spencer answered.

After I wiped down the counters, I flipped the switch on the coffeemaker and emptied the dishwater from the sink. We'd spent New Year's Day with my father. Jane, his new girlfriend, was working at the hospital, and I felt bad that he'd be alone. It was easier now that Dad had given Spencer and me his blessing to date. Things had seemed to improve between the three of us since the holiday party Spencer had held for his clients.

I worked diligently to put the dishes away, while my father and Spencer retired into the living room. They'd thrown on a replay of the most recent hockey game and now sat shouting at the TV. I giggled, listening to them banter back and forth as I pulled three plates out of the cupboard and cut three pieces of cake for dessert, and then I waited for the coffee to finish perking while silently humming a song to myself.

I heard laughter coming from the other room, and I smiled. It was nice to see them getting along again. It was also nice not to have to sneak around anymore. Once that happened, not only did my relationship improve with my father, but so did theirs. They were back to speaking again and going out for wings and beer on game nights.

However, while that was good for now, my dad still didn't have any idea about the baby or our engagement. We'd decided not to tell him everything at once. Spencer had told me he wanted to ask my father's permission to marry me, but we agreed not to tell him about the baby until later. Besides, it was too early to say anything. My family doctor figured I was only maybe four weeks along and we didn't want him to think we were having some shotgun wedding because I was pregnant.

I'd just pulled mugs down from the cupboard when I felt Spencer wrap his arms around me from behind and pull me against him. "Need any help?" he questioned, kissing the side of my neck.

"I think I got it," I said, placing my hand on his muscular forearm. "You haven't said anything to him yet have you?" I questioned while closing my eyes as he kissed my neck again.

"I promised you I'd wait until you are in the living room with me." Spencer placed a kiss on my shoulder and chuckled. "Don't you trust me?"

I smiled and said, "I trust you," while spinning in his arms and kissing him.

He wrapped his arms around me, kissing me a little harder, his tongue parting my lips and meeting mine, while his hands cupped my ass. The second our lips parted, I leaned my head against his chest, breathing hard. I could already feel his hard cock pressing into me.

"You better calm that down." I giggled.

"I could take you right here, right now." He whispered and let out a chuckle while adjusting himself. "Anything I can help you with?"

"Could you take the cake in?"

"I can," he said, grabbing my ass and kissing me one more time before picking up the three plates.

I poured two cups of coffee and filled my mug with hot water from the kettle, plopping in a tea bag. Then I put the three mugs on the small tray and carried them into the living room.

"This looks fantastic," my father said, taking a bite of the double fudge chocolate cake I'd made. "I've been missing your baking around here."

I smiled. "Dad, anytime you want anything, just ask me. I'm more than happy to make you something."

I'd basically moved out and in with Spencer the second Dad had said we could date. I kept some of my things at the house here, and occasionally to please my father, I came back home for a night. Those nights were few because it was easier to be with Spencer since the morning sickness had struck me hard.

"I'm so glad you are feeling better. That flu you had really hit you bad," Dad said.

I looked at Spencer out of the corner of my eye. His eyes met mine for a split second. "Yeah, it was a bad one," Spencer bit out.

"Looks like you lost a lot of weight, too," Dad replied, giving me a once over.

"You think I've lost weight?" I questioned, looking down at myself. "I don't think I have." I shrugged, trying to play it off.

"No, neither do I," Spencer said.

"Well, I do, but don't worry, you'll put it back on in no time," Dad said. "You always lost weight when you got the flu."

I glanced again at Spencer, who sat there watching me. Then he sat forward. "So, Jon, how are things with Jane?"

"Good, very good. We are looking at planning a trip in the coming weeks."

"Great. That is exciting. Things must be going well then between you two."

"Yes, so well, in fact, that I put my Finding Forever profile on pause. I hope that is okay."

Spencer nodded. "Of course. That is why we have that feature."

"I'm glad you guys are getting along so well. She seems nice. Maybe someone that I could bond with," I said, hoping that maybe one day she might be like a mother to me.

"She really likes you, Ainsley. It would be nice if you guys got to know one another a little better," Dad said.

The room grew quiet. My body seemed to be filled with tension as I took a small bite of my cake. My stomach turned. I just wished Spencer would get on with this and ask him already.

"What about you two?" my father asked. "Things all right?"

I could tell my father cared but really didn't want to know any details. It had been hard on him to start when he'd found us in bed together. It had been hard on all of us, and that had almost ripped Spencer and me apart from one another for good.

"Things are going better than expected," Spencer said. "That's why we wanted to talk to you about something." Spencer set his plate down and placed his hand on my knee, giving me a gentle squeeze.

"Oh," my father said, taking the last bite of his cake and washing it down with coffee. Then he looked up at us, then down to where Spencer's hand now rested on my inner thigh. My nerves were so bad that I had to set my plate down to stop shaking. "Well, what is it?"

I blew out a breath as Spencer took over the conversation. "As you know, I'm really in love with your daughter, and she is with me."

My father looked at the pair of us, not saying a word. I feared this was going to be another blowup, and I bit my bottom lip and wrapped my arm through Spencer's, while my father sat there watching my every move.

"I've given things considerable thought and, well, I'd like to ask you for permission to marry her."

I'd lowered my eyes as Spencer had spoken. I'd was afraid to look and see my father's reaction because I feared it was going to be the same as the night he'd caught us. I wouldn't be able to take that, and I prayed that wasn't what was coming. The only sound in the room was from the game on TV. I hated the silence and I wanted someone to say something. I shyly glanced up to see my father staring at us both.

"Married?" My father cleared his throat.

"Yes, sir," Spencer answered, his voice calm and even, never once faltering.

"Ainsley, what do you think about this?"

Spencer and I hadn't gone over what would happen if

he asked me anything. All Spencer had said was not to worry, that he'd handle it because he knew how nervous I was.

When I didn't answer him, my father cleared his throat again. "Ainsley, I asked you a question."

"Daddy, we want your permission. I've said it before. I'm in love with Spencer. I'm happy. I want to spend the rest of my life with him."

My father grew quiet, sitting there looking at us. Then, without another word, he got up and wandered down the hall to his bedroom. I looked over at Spencer, who sat there looking at me with the same perplexed look on his face.

He'd been gone for a few minutes, and I was about to say something to Spencer when my father returned to the living room and looked at us both. "I knew this day would come, eventually. Given the brief history with the pair of you, I already know you won't take no for an answer, so I'll give you my blessing."

I couldn't believe what my father had said, but I wrapped my arms around Spencer and hugged him tight.

"Spencer, just make sure you take care of my baby girl."

Spencer let me go and looked up at my father. "Jon, you know I will." He stood up and shook my father's hand.

Relief flooded me as I stood up and hugged my father

tightly. "Thank you, Dad." I whispered in his ear. Then the three of us sat back down, but not before I pulled the ring Spencer had surprised me with from my purse so I could show the only person in my life who had always been there for me, until now.

Ainsley

I stood in the bedroom looking at my reflection in the mirror, turning to the right and then the left, and again looking forward. "I don't know about this dress. It just doesn't seem to hang right," I cried. "I knew I should have gotten the one I was looking at the other night, but it was so expensive."

"Don't worry, you look fabulous," Carly answered, not paying attention to anything I'd said as she lay across our bed, flipping through one of our favourite magazines.

"I don't know." I smoothed the fabric of the dress down my body. "This one just doesn't hang right."

Carly closed the magazine and rolled onto her back. "Ainsley, it's just the engagement party. What difference does it make? You've worn that dress plenty of times before, and you weren't picky about the way it hung."

I shrugged. "Well, it matters to me now." I slid the dress off and put my jeans and T-shirt back on. "I just want everything to be perfect." I sat down on the edge of the bed beside Carly just as Nikki walked into the bedroom.

"I know, but seriously, it's only a small gathering of a few people."

"Yeah, only a few people." I giggled, thinking about all the invitations I'd sent out.

"Ainsley, can I have dessert now?"

"Sure, bug, let's go," I said, putting my hand on her head and leading her out of mine and Spencer's room. Carly let out a sigh and got up, following behind us.

"What kind of ice cream do you want? Chocolate, vanilla, or strawberry?"

Nikki put her forefinger to her lips. "Mmmm, chocolate and strawberry," she said, her eyes lighting up.

I shook my head and placed my hand on my hip. "No, one or the other."

"Mmmm..." Nikki thought hard for a moment and then yelled, "Chocolate with syrup and sprinkles!"

I laughed as I turned and pulled a bowl down from the cupboard, while Nikki climbed up on a stool beside Carly and watched as I plopped a scoop of ice cream into her bowl.

"Anyway, back to what we were talking about earlier.

Now I'm being serious, and I want a serious answer. Picture your life for me for just a moment?"

"I am picturing it. I'm happy, Carly," I said, drizzling chocolate syrup onto the ice cream in Nikki's bowl, then covering it with pink and white sprinkles.

"I don't mean now. Yes, sure, you're happy now. You have all the warm and fuzzy feelings of being in a rather new relationship. I mean, think about your future."

I put the lid back on the ice cream container and shoved it in the freezer. "I am thinking about the future! We have Nikki and two other babies. This one, and perhaps a little boy, who looks just like Spencer."

"A brother and a sister!" Nikki exclaimed, taking the bowl from me. "I thought you said there was only one baby in there? Two can't possibly fit in there?" she said, pointing to my flat stomach.

Carly looked at Nikki and mouthed to me, "She knows?"

"Nikki, eat your ice cream," I said, knowing full well we shouldn't be talking about any of this in front of her.

"She only knows because she heard Spencer and I talking about it and asked. Spencer doesn't believe in not telling her. So, we sat her down and told her that one day she would have a little brother or sister," I whispered to Carly.

"I see. Well, regardless, two others? You are nuts. And I'm talking distant future. He's all hot now, but what do you think he is going to look like in, say, twenty years?" she said, keeping her voice low.

"Can I go into the living room and colour?" Nikki asked, grinning at me.

"Sure, just don't spill, okay? Keep everything at your little table."

"I will." She grinned, shoving a spoonful of ice cream in her mouth. "Bye, Carly."

"Bye." We both watched as she carefully carried the bowl into the living room with two hands, leaving the two of us in the kitchen. "Now seriously? What about twenty years from now? What do you think it will be like then?"

"God! What are any of us going to look like in twenty years?" I cried.

"I'm being serious! You'll only be forty, but he'll be sixty," she said, scrunching her nose up in disgust.

"So am I being serious. Now please, I am marrying Spencer. I'm happy, I'm excited, and it would be nice for my best friend to be excited for me as well."

"You say that now."

"She says what now?" Carly jumped at the sound of Spencer's voice as he poked his head around the corner.

"Nothing," I immediately said, looking at Carly letting her know the conversation was ending.

He stepped into the kitchen carrying a suit bag. He made his way over to me, put his arm around me, and kissed the side of my neck.

"Hey," I said, meeting his lips. "See that you picked up your suit from the cleaner. I meant to do that right after I left the office today, but Carly called, and I forgot." I shrugged.

"Don't worry about it, but no, this isn't my suit. I made a stop after work. This is for you." He held up the suit bag and lowered the zipper. It shocked me to see the champagne-coloured dress I wished I'd bought when I'd tried it on at a little boutique outside of town last weekend. I'd wanted it for our engagement party, but after seeing the price, I had decided against it.

"What is this?" I questioned. "Tell me you didn't," I cried with excitement as I removed the bag from the hanger.

"I did." He grinned. "You looked...mmm...well, it's not suitable to say how you looked in it the other day in front of a guest," he said, leaning in a biting my earlobe.

"Oh God, save me," Carly said, sticking her finger down her throat and pretending to gag.

"Not in front of little eyes," I whispered as Nikki stood before us, holding her empty bowl.

I smiled as I took the dress from Spencer, while he took the bowl from Nikki, wiping her mouth with a paper towel before he picked her up and threw her in the air. "How's my baby girl?"

Nikki let out a squeal, followed by a laugh as Spencer

held her up over his head. "Put me down, Daddy," she squealed.

Spencer put her down and watched as she ran off into the other room. He walked over to the table and sorted through the pile of mail I'd left there.

"Oh, and we got a couple more RSVPs in the mail today for the engagement party," I said, showing Carly the dress.

"Was one of them from my brother, Max?"

I shook my head. "No, have not heard from him yet. I can call him tomorrow if you'd like? Today was the last day to respond."

"I'll take care of Max. I've got to call him tonight about work," he said, leaning in and kissing me before he made his way down the hall to his office.

I smiled as I looked at Carly, excitement filling me as I looked at the dress. "Come, let's try this one on."

"I sure hope this dress hangs better." Carly giggled, following behind me.

Spencer

"Spencer Brooks is getting remarried. Never thought I'd live to see the day," my older brother, Mike, said as Ainsley and I approached him and his wife, Trina.

"Hey, Trina, Mike. Enjoying yourselves?"

"Yes, everything is wonderful. The food is fantastic, and these little appetizers are amazing," Trina said, holding up one of my favourites, Cranberry Pecan Goat Cheese Truffles. "You did a fantastic job organizing everything, Ainsley. And this dress... is just gorgeous on you."

Trina and Mike had met through Finding Forever. They'd been the first successful match that Spencer's company had, and Mike had been the reason Spencer had started the company.

"Thanks." Ainsley smiled and leaned into my side as I

looked around the room. Everyone seemed to have a good time, but a huge part of me felt tense. As I skimmed the room, I noticed Carly staring over at us as she talked to her date. Whatever she said caused him and another one of Ainsley's other friends to turn our way and watch us as well, whispering to one another.

I was about to turn back to the conversation with my brother when I noticed Jon and Jane standing off to the side. They both held a glass of wine, talking amongst themselves, neither looking thrilled. Carly moved over to them and whispered something. Both Jon and Jane laughed, then they both looked over in our direction with an odd expression.

I felt as if I were becoming paranoid, as I never usually cared about what people thought, but after hearing Carly talking to Ainsley about our age difference the other day, and trying to give her reasons that we shouldn't get married, I worried she was now having second thoughts and had said something to someone, which was why we were getting all the looks. I searched my mind, trying to remember if she'd given me any sign of that, but she hadn't.

I glanced over toward where I'd last seen Nikki playing with some other children, but she wasn't there. Panic filled me for a moment as I searched the crowd until I spotted her with Brittany, pulling on the bottom of her dress to get her attention. Brittany ignored her because she was glaring at us from across the room. I knew the look on her face well, and it clearly wasn't one of happiness, although that would be a look I wouldn't recognize anymore, anyway. I hadn't wanted her here, but she'd insisted on bringing Nikki instead of just allowing us to have her for the night.

"Ainsley, how's things going for you at Spencer's office?" Mike asked.

I felt Ainsley grip my side a little tighter, and I turned my attention back to the conversation. "Things are going well. I'm enjoying my position very much."

"Good. My brother is treating you well then? I've heard he can be a hard man to work for."

"Mike, stop it," Trina said, jabbing his side.

"She knows I'm kidding. Don't you?" Mike said, winking.

Ainsley smiled and rested her head on my shoulder as the four of us laughed. I glanced around the room one more time, looking for our younger brother. "Mike, have you seen Max yet?" I questioned.

My brother shook his head. "Not yet. I didn't even hear from him to know if he was coming or not. I called, but there was no answer. It's just like Max, wrapped up in his own affairs all the time. Been that way his entire life."

I chuckled. "Yep, neither did we. Guess that is the

thanks I get for giving him the Denver branch of Finding Forever to run." I shrugged.

Handing over the Denver branch to my brother had been a hard decision for me. After all, I'd built this company, with no help from anyone. I'd originally planned to spend half my time in Denver and the other half here, until I'd found out about the pregnancy. I wasn't comfortable leaving Ainsley alone now, after we spent a few nights talking about it, and even though she told me that whatever I decided, she'd support, I knew I didn't want to be far from here. I looked at other options. There were many, but I knew Max needed some help. I just didn't want to end up regretting the decision.

"Give him a chance. Perhaps something came up last minute at work?"

"That would be hard to believe. The soft launch is next week. Right now, it's basically employee training week. If something has come up already, we may be in trouble." I swallowed hard. I wasn't that much of a control freak, but Max also didn't have the best track record, and giving him some control over this made me nervous.

"So, how are the plans coming for the wedding?" Trina questioned. "Do we have a venue yet?"

I wrapped my arm around Ainsley tighter, waiting for her to answer.

"Good. We are still waiting to hear from the venues, and I am currently trying to set things up with a couple of caterers and, of course, bakers for the cake. This week is a big week though. I am going shopping for a wedding dress," Ainsley whispered, like it was a secret.

"Very exciting. If you'd like, I will send you a list of stores to check out."

"Oh, please," Ainsley said, smiling up at me. "It would help me a lot."

"I will. Why don't you call me this weekend and I'll give you a list."

"Thank you, I will do that. I am looking for a certain dress, and I'm hoping one store here will carry the designer I am looking for."

"Send me the designer and I will see what I can find out."

"All right, Ainsley, we should get moving. We have many more people to talk to before the night is over. Can we catch up with you in a little while?" I asked.

"Sure thing, and if I see Max, I'll let him know you are looking for him."

Mike shook my hand, while Ainsley hugged Trina. Then we quickly switched before making our way to the next couple.

Ainsley was lounging on the couch in one of my T-shirts when I came into the living room carrying a glass of water for her and a scotch on the rocks for me. I was looking forward to relaxing with her. We finally had the house to ourselves for the weekend.

"Here you go."

"Thank you. God, I really wish I could have a glass of wine," She muttered, resting her head on a pillow.

"Everything okay?" I questioned, sitting down beside her and pulling her bare foot into my lap, giving her a gentle massage.

She let out a breath and closed her eyes, relaxing farther into the couch. "I don't know. Tonight just didn't feel as fun as I thought it would. It seemed like everyone was staring and whispering. To be honest, all I felt was tension."

"I know what you mean. At one point, I thought it was just my imagination, but I got that feeling as well. Also, I am certain, at one point, I heard Carly whisper to one of your mutual friends something about 'wrinkled old balls,'" I said, taking a sip of my scotch and placing the glass back down.

She giggled. "I'm sorry. She's still so hung up on the

age difference. It's not a secret that she has never really approved of us. To be honest, I think she was more shocked when I found out I was pregnant than I was."

We both grew quiet as I continued rubbing her foot, digging into all the places I knew she loved. My mind was still reeling from the ball comment, and I hoped Ainsley didn't feel that way. The more I tried to put it out of my mind, the more it kept gnawing at me. "Ainsley?"

"Hmmm?" She opened her sleepy eyes and looked at me.

"Do you think that?" I questioned.

"Think what?"

"That my balls are old and wrinkled?" I asked, trying my best to keep a straight face.

Ainsley was serious for a moment, and then she burst into laughter. "I'm sorry... I can't answer that."

I laughed as well, but not because it was funny; it was more because I was relieved to see her expression change. "Sorry, I couldn't help that. After hearing you and her talk the other night, I was worried that perhaps she was convincing you to leave, to find someone younger."

"It's okay. Never worry, I will always love your balls."

"I'm glad." I chuckled.

"Seriously though, Spencer, a younger man couldn't even hold a candle to you. I see how these guys treat Carly, and to be honest, I think I'd lose my mind. It's all games with them, and when she's told me about the sex, well..."

"What does she say?"

"That none of them last and that most of them are more concerned with getting themselves off and not worrying about her."

"Ah, yes, well, that comes with age and maturity. As for lasting, well, there are times I can barely hold it together with you."

"Oh." Her cheeks flushed, "It was nice to see Mike and Trina there. They seemed to really be happy for us." She said, changing the subject.

"Yes, Mike was thrilled when I told him, albeit a little surprised, but only because he never thought I'd marry again after Brittany."

"Can't say I blame you there. Did you see the way she was glaring at us tonight?"

"How could I not? I also couldn't help but notice how she was ignoring Nikki as well. I really didn't want her to go home with her tonight, but it is her turn to have her. Besides, I think we could both use some alone time."

"I know. At one point, Nikki came to me to take her to the bathroom. I was worried Brittany might follow us into the bathroom and bitch me out, but when we came back out, I found her flirting with Paul, head of tech support. I don't even thing she noticed Nikki had come to me."

"If that ever happens again, you need to come and get me right away. She will not ignore the needs of my daughter to satisfy her own. I've been fighting her on that for years."

Ainsley nodded and then rested her head back against the pillow as I continued rubbing her foot, then switching to the other one. "You might want to warn poor Paul, too."

"Noted."

"Can I talk to you about something?" Ainsley whispered, placing her hand on my forearm.

"Of course. What is it?"

Ainsley blew out a breath before beginning. "The other day, while I was in putting Nikki's clothes away, I realized we don't have a separate bedroom for the baby. So, Nikki will have to share her room when she is here."

"You know, I was thinking the same thing myself. I was planning to bring this up to you later in the week. What would you say to finding a place of our own?"

"What do you mean?" Ainsley questioned. "This one is our own."

"No, this place isn't one we chose together. This is the house I chose after my divorce. I needed a place to live, and I needed to have room for Nikki so I could bring her here on my weekends. We are clearly going to outgrow this place, and I thought it might be nice to find a place that we can build together."

Ainsley nodded. "Where would we look?"

"Well, on my way home the other night, I drove

through a neighborhood close to here, just a few blocks over. The houses are bigger, which means we'd have another bedroom or two. Plus, if we plan it right from the start, perhaps I could also fit an office in. That way I can work from home if need be and help you when the baby comes."

I watched as she thought for a moment. "Were there any houses for sale?"

"There were a couple that I saw. I can make an appointment with an agent to see them. See if we like any of them. There is no harm in looking."

I watched her eyes light up while the idea I'd planted floated through her mind. I wanted her to have everything she wanted, things I knew were important to her. Over the last few weeks, she asked me if it was okay if she made some subtle changes around the house. I kept telling her she didn't need my permission, but she still came to me. I knew she'd never come out and say she wanted a place she could make her own, but I knew it was on her mind.

"Don't be afraid to tell me how you feel, Ainsley."

She shrugged. "It might be nice to have someplace we can call our own. I know that eventually I won't think of this as just your place, though. It's just going to take me some time."

"I'll call the agent this week and set something up." I smiled, picking up my drink and taking a sip. Ainsley smiled and then closed her eyes while I continued rubbing her feet, and she sank farther into the couch cushions as she relaxed. I grabbed the remote and turned the radio on, soft jazz music floating through the air.

I loved these quiet times with her. There was something about being with her that brought out a fire in my soul. She had made me feel alive when, most of these past few years, I felt dead inside.

Ainsley

"Nikki's dinner is in the fridge on her favourite plate. Hopefully, that will make it easier for you to get her to eat tonight. All you need to do is take it out and heat it in the microwave. Reheat it for about three minutes. She will try to tell you she can eat in the living room, but she needs to eat at the table. Spencer thinks she is getting away with too much at Brittany's, so he is implementing stricter rules for when she is here. She's been horrible since she returned."

"What about drinks?"

"She can have a juice box or a glass of milk, whichever she wants. Don't let her con you into giving her pop. It gets her crazy hyper, and lately she has been sneaky about that, too."

"Okay, plate, no pop, and at the table. I think I got it," Carly said, hopping up onto the counter.

"Oh, and I got out some construction paper and some new markers. She wanted to do some arts and crafts tonight. I believe she wanted to make Spencer a birthday card. She needs to do that at the table as well, since we found a minor cut on the couch the other day that we had to have repaired."

Carly nodded and then took a sip of the pop I'd gotten for her. "No problem. I'll help her with that. Maybe I'll even make Spencer one." She winked.

I laughed, imagining what Carly would put inside the card. I shook my head as I reached up into the cupboard and grabbed a box of crackers, put five on the plate, and then grabbed the cheese from the fridge and began making Nikki a snack before we left. I had just added a handful of grapes when Carly cleared her throat.

"Don't you find this a little weird?"

"Find what weird?" I asked.

"I dunno, this. You used to be the babysitter, and now here he is, hiring a babysitter."

I looked at Carly, who wore a smug smile on her face. "I am a former babysitter. Currently, I am a personal assistant."

"Ooh, I forgot. You've moved up in the world." Carly giggled.

"Don't make fun of me. You know one day you too could end up not babysitting and spending time in corporate America." I laughed.

"I don't think so. I'll be living the wild life, working with young kids in a school somewhere, not in corporate America under my boss's desk!"

"You bitch!" My mouth dropped open, and we both laughed. I shoved Carly's shoulder just as Nikki walked into the kitchen and placed a few sheets of construction paper on the table.

"Carly, if you give me two desserts, I'll tell my dad nice things about you." Then she turned and looked at me with a smile.

I looked back at her, trying not to laugh, and was about to say something when Carly interjected.

"If I give you two desserts, you'll be sick, and unfortunately I don't do puke, so..."

Nikki hung her head, and then, almost as if Carly had said nothing, she looked up at me with hope in her eyes. "Will you and Daddy be back in time for dessert?"

"Mmmm, I'm not too sure. We might be, but to be on the safe side, you should have dessert when Carly gives it to you."

"But Mom lets me have two," Nikki cried.

I glanced at Carly and shook my head. This was totally abnormal behaviour for Nikki, and I was glad when I heard Spencer's voice from the hallway.

"Well then, maybe you shouldn't have any," he said, coming around the corner dressed in jeans and a sweater. The scent of his cologne combined with the sound of domination in his voice made my knees weak. "Ready to go?"

I nodded.

"Carly, please. Can I have two desserts?" Nikki questioned as she climbed up on the kitchen chair.

Spencer looked at me and smiled. "What did Ainsley tell Carly?" Spencer questioned.

"She said maybe."

Spencer looked over at me and then back to Nikki. "No, I don't think she did. Now you behave yourself for Carly, and if there is mention of two desserts again, I will tell Carly you can't have any. We've got to get going," Spencer said, placing a kiss on the top of Nikki's head.

"Awww, Daddy," Nikki cried.

"Call us if you need anything," I whispered to Carly, then I hugged her. "Thank you for doing this."

"No problem. Have fun house hunting!" Carly called before sitting down beside Nikki, distracting her from us leaving while helping her cut the paper.

We had seen two houses already, and now were just pulling into the driveway of the third. Immediately, I could see us living in this one. The front of the house was beautifully landscaped, and I was already in love with the wrap-around porch. Spencer cut the engine, and we climbed out of the car just as our agent pulled in behind us.

"All right, so this one has four bedrooms, 2.5 baths, and a fully landscaped backyard complete with a pool and hot tub," Nick said, walking with us up to the front door and unlocking it. "It's also currently empty, so that means there is way more flexibility on the move-in date," he said as he opened the door.

We stepped inside, and immediately I fell in love. The entire house had been renovated, and they had turned one bedroom into an office, complete with built-in shelves and a desk. We walked through the entire house, then went into the backyard, which was beautiful.

"Nick, could you leave us alone for a few minutes? Give us a chance to speak in private?" Spencer questioned, shoving his phone back into his pocket.

"Sure, of course. I'll be in the kitchen," Nick responded.

The back door closed, and Spencer and I stood alone in the backyard. I hadn't been able to read Spencer's thoughts at all as we'd walked through each of the homes. It would have been easier had I been able to. At least I would have known not to get my hopes up.

"Well?" he questioned, coming over to me. "Thoughts?"

Immediately, my stomach knotted. I didn't know if he liked any of them, and I certainly didn't want to be the one who decided. This was supposed to be a joint decision. This house, though, was perfect.

"Did you like any of them?" I asked.

"I did. I'd like you to share your thoughts with me. I want to know what you think!"

Spencer had done all the work. He'd contacted Nick, he'd booked the appointments, he'd chosen the houses to look at. I had no clue how much any of them even were, or what we could afford, but each of them would have fit my father's house and Spencer's current house inside of them at least four times. I let out a sigh and shifted my weight from one foot to the other.

"Do we need to keep looking?" he questioned.

I'd been quiet the entire afternoon, doing my best to hide my excitement in any of the houses we'd been in. "I don't know."

"You don't know?" Spencer questioned. "From the look on your face walking through this place, I was sure you'd have attacked me by now and told me to get this one." Spencer shrugged. "I guess I'll tell Nick to keep searching." He turned to head back inside.

"How did you know I loved this one?" I questioned, just as Spencer placed his hand on the doorknob.

Spencer walked over to me and pulled me into his arms. "There have only been a handful of times I've seen that look on your face. You know, the one you have when you are completely in love with something... or someone," he said, bringing his hand to my cheek before he leaned in and met my lips with his. "The one that is on your face right this minute, actually," he whispered, nipping at my lower lip.

"Oh, I didn't know I had a look." I could feel the heat rise to my cheeks.

"It's the same look you get when I kiss my way down your body..." he murmured, running his fingers down my side to where my shirt met the waist of my jeans, his fingers grazing my bare skin.

I closed my eyes. "Stop it," I whispered, grabbing his hand as a shiver of excitement ran through my body. "Concentrate." I giggled.

"Oh, I am concentrating," he whispered in my ear, the feel of his breath sending chills through me. "Shall we put an offer in?"

I pulled out of his arms and looked around the backyard. The house was perfect, and it would accommodate our family nicely. "How much is it?" I questioned.

"That is not something you need to worry about. All I need to know is a yes or a no."

I nodded my head and smiled, excitement building inside of me. "Put an offer in," I said, leaning in and meeting his lips.

"Okay, I'll go talk to Nick. Call Carly and make sure

everything is going okay with Nikki. Let her know that once we finish here that we are going out to celebrate."

We stood at the hostess desk at The Porterhouse restaurant, waiting to be seated. Spencer had worked with Nick to come up with an offer on the house, and once they had finished, Nick told us we would hear from him soon.

"Was Nikki behaving when you called?" Spencer questioned as we waited.

"Yes, Carly said she only asked for double dessert three more times." I giggled.

"That child. I'm going to have to talk to Brittany about her behaviour. However, I remember when she pulled that on you the first couple of times you watched her."

"Yeah, only I fell for it because someone didn't warn me. This is different though. Her attitude toward everything is bad." I shrugged.

Spencer pulled me to his side. "I'll talk to Nikki and Brittany. However, what can I say? Kids will be kids." He chuckled.

"Right this way, Mr. Brooks," the hostess said, grabbing two menus before leading the way to the table.

We'd been seated for about ten minutes when we heard a familiar voice greet us at the table. Spencer's eyes met mine, and we both looked up at the same time to see his ex-wife, Brittany, holding an order pad.

"Well, well, if it isn't my two most favourite people in the entire world, my ex-husband and the slutty babysitter." She sneered.

I swallowed hard and looked at Spencer, who sat there looking at her with a straight face. I'd seen this exact face before, at the office the other day when he had a meeting with an employee who had broken company rules. It hadn't ended pretty, and I suspected this little interaction wouldn't end well either.

"Brittany, I'll care for you not to allow personal issues to interfere with your job," he said, clearing his throat.

"Who the fuck are you? My boss?" she whispered. "I'll care for you not to allow personal issues to interfere with your job," she mimicked.

Immediately, I saw where Nikki's behaviour was coming from, and I glanced to Spencer to see if he recognized it too. Spencer looked at me out of the corner of his eye.

"We'll both have the fillet, baked potato with a side of mushrooms for myself, and asparagus for Ainsley. And two waters," he said, closing the menu and grabbing mine, handing them both to Brittany.

She glared at him. "Still ordering for the woman, I see. Does she not have a mouth?"

I lowered my eyes to the table when I felt her steely stare on me.

"Oh wait, of course she does, otherwise you'd never would have fucked her."

I could still feel her stare. I wanted to hide; her words mortified me.

"Brittany," Spencer said through his clenched jaw.

With a smirk on her face, she marched off and across the restaurant.

"Oh God, Spencer, I can't do this. Can we please just leave?"

Spencer shook his head. "You can do this. You're stronger than her. She is trying to get me to cause a scene in here. I didn't know she worked here. She probably got a job here because she knows this is where I do most of my lunch meetings with the executives. I was late one day when I dropped Nikki off and I mentioned it to her. Since she knows that, she also knows this would be the worst place for me to lose my patience."

"I know. I just can't do this." I could feel the tears burning behind my eyes. "I can't have her say things like that about me."

He reached across the table and took my hand in his.

He was about to say something when two glasses of water were dropped onto the table in front of us, and I glanced up to see Brittany once again glaring at me.

"Where is our daughter, Spencer?" she said, placing her hands on her hips.

"At home... with a sitter." Spencer met my eyes, reassuring me with a look.

"Oh, how convenient. You know you really have a thing for babysitters, don't you? Let me ask you, are you screwing her as well?"

I glanced over at Spencer. His jaw was tight, and I could see the vein in the side of his neck throbbing. The look on his face was one of pure anger. I'd never seen him like this. I gripped his hand a little tighter to remind him of where we were when someone called out to Brittany. She whipped around and took off over to another table.

"Are you okay?" I questioned, as I noticed he'd followed her movements.

"She is just doing this to get at me. I won't lie, it's working."

"Perhaps you should speak to the manager," I suggested, not wanting Spencer to take matters into his own hands and lose his temper.

"Oh, I plan on that," Spencer said, gripping my hand tighter as he stopped a server walking by the table, asking to speak with the manager.

"I'm just going to use the washroom," I mumbled as I stood up.

"It's over there," Spencer said, nodding in the washroom's direction.

"I'll be right back."

I'd taken a few moments to gather myself before I opened the door to the stall and approached the sink. I ran my hands under the warm water and lathered the soap as I looked at myself in the mirror. I could see the tension and worry on my face. I let out a breath and grabbed a paper towel to dry my hands. I pulled my mascara from my purse and was about to apply it when the door to the washroom opened. My heart started to pound when I saw Brittany walk in.

She said nothing. I frowned as I watched her bend down and look under the stalls. Then she turned to me. Her eyes ran the length of my body before they met mine.

"You think Spencer is marrying you because he loves you, don't you?"

I stood there, my heart racing as she waited for my response. When I said nothing, she let out a small laugh.

"I thought the same thing when I was pregnant with Nikki. Boy, was I wrong. Don't get too comfortable, because when the next best thing comes along, Spencer will be gone."

"That's not true," I said, my voice cracking.

"It's not? Let me guess, he isn't interested in anyone else. He only wants you to be happy and secure."

I blinked hard. I could feel the tears burning behind my eyes as her words hit me. Words Spencer himself had said to me time and time again.

"You'll find out. Trust me."

I wanted to fire back at her. I wanted to ask her if she didn't want me to have him, then why did she cheat on him? I stood there, courage growing inside me and just as I was about to, the door opened, and a woman came walking in. She stopped in her tracks and looked at both of us clearly sensing the tension between us. I looked at the woman, and that was when I dashed out the door. I made my way over to the table where Spencer stood speaking with, I assumed, the manager. I slid into my seat and wiped my eyes.

"What is it?" Spencer demanded. The gentlemen he was speaking with turned and looked at me.

"It's nothing," I whispered, wiping my eyes again without looking at Spencer.

"She approached you, didn't she?" he questioned. "In the bathroom." Anger lined Spencer's face.

I looked up to meet Spencer's eyes, only to see that he and the man he'd been speaking to were now looking over toward the washrooms, just in time to see Brittany step out onto the floor. She made brief eye contact with them before she cleared an empty table.

"I'll take care of it, Spencer," the man said, shaking his hand. "Again, I am sorry about this. Please enjoy your meal tonight. It's on the house."

Within seconds, the manager had pulled Brittany from the floor. Spencer looked at me, worry lining his face. "I'm sorry about this," he said. "Now, what did she say to you?"

It took me only a few seconds before a tear escaped my eyes. I knew deep in my heart that what she said wasn't true. I knew their past; I knew why they'd divorced, but what I didn't know was why Brittany was doing this. I decided not to tell Spencer what she'd said. I just wished this was going to be the last time I ever laid eyes on Brittany.

Spencer

I was exhausted as I sat at my desk going over reports the next morning. It had been a long and somewhat stressful night for the pair of us after we'd returned from dinner. I'd put Nikki to bed, while Ainsley had crawled into the soaker tub and had a hot bath. Afterward, we'd sat up late, talking about what had happened with Brittany at the restaurant. Ainsley had burst into tears many times as I tried to get her to talk to me about what Brittany said in the washroom, but she refused to tell me. Instead, I could only imagine all the cruel things she'd said, and even though she assured me she knew what Brittany told her wasn't true, I was still upset that I wasn't able to defend myself. She finally curled up in my arms and fell asleep, but I stayed awake for hours, staring at the ceiling.

I heard a soft knock on my office door. I looked up to

see Ainsley holding a steaming cup of coffee, a soft smile on her face.

"You are a godsend," I said, throwing down the report I'd been going over as she set the mug down on the warming plate she'd gotten me last week, after I'd complained that I kept drinking cold coffee.

She said nothing. Instead, she nodded and turned, heading toward the door.

"Ainsley? Is everything okay?" I questioned.

"Yep." She smiled, but I knew it wasn't a real one. She appeared to be far more upset than she was when we'd left for the office this morning and that concerned me.

"Ainsley, shut my door and come over here."

She stopped. I watched as she clenched her fists at her side and then shut the door and approached my desk. "What?" she demanded, crossing her arms in front of her chest, completely closing me off.

I pushed my chair away from my desk and studied her. "Come over here," I said, nodding to the space between me and the desk.

She let out a sigh and reluctantly walked over to me, wedging herself between me and my desk. She leaned against it and looked down at me. "What is it?"

"I think I'm the one who should ask you that."

She let out a deep sigh. "There were messages for me this morning... from Brittany," she said through clenched teeth, her eyes glistening with tears.

"I see. Why didn't you forward them to me?" I asked, doing my best to remain calm. I'd had it with that woman.

"Just better to delete them." She shrugged. "No need for the both of us to hear her cruel words." She looked away so I could no longer see her eyes.

I shook my head and placed my hands on her hips. "No, you should have sent them to me."

"Did you know she got fired last night?" she questioned. "She left that in one message and how she blames me for it."

I nodded. "I knew. She deserved it."

"I know, but in her message, she is blaming me."

"That is ridiculous. She deserved it, and you know it."

Ainsley slowly nodded her head and wiped her eyes.

"Ainsley, I want to know what else is bothering you."

I studied her face. Her eyes watered, and soon they filled with tears and she broke down. She brought her hands up to her face and sobbed into them. I placed my hands on her hips and rested my head on her abdomen. I closed my eyes and felt her fingers run through my hair.

"All of this just hurts so much," she cried.

"All of what? Brittany? Don't give her that kind of power."

I watched as she wiped the tears from her eyes. "Everything, Spencer. The venues won't call us back. My best friend keeps asking me to think about what it will be like to be married to you in twenty years, and your ex-wife hates me. I still don't have a dress. It's just..." She let out a huge sob.

"Brittany hates me too. Honestly, I think she hates herself as well as everyone else." I chuckled as I pulled her onto my lap and leaned back in my chair, pulling her into my chest.

"It just seems like she is...dare I say it... jealous."

"Ha, she can be jealous. Remember, it was I who found another man between her legs. She has no right to be jealous or to say a damn word about us."

"I know."

"You know what I think?"

"What's that?"

"That most of this is all just baby hormones. Take a breath..." I said in a calm voice as I ran my fingers through her hair and looked her in the eyes.

"No, it's not." She sniffled.

"Oh, I think it is. You aren't this sensitive, that much I know. Perhaps it would be a good idea for you to take a day off. I think you need to be by yourself to relax. It's been a lot, yes, but it's not as bad as you're thinking," I said in a low voice.

"It's not?"

I shook my head. "No, we've only had a call into a couple of venues for a week. I'm not worried. Everything is going to work out fine. I promise. As for the calls from Brittany, I will block her number from your extension. I will direct all her calls to me and me only. As for Carly, well, she'll learn when she meets someone."

Ainsley met my eyes, leaned in, and kissed me softly on the lips, while running her fingers through my hair. "Thank you," she whispered.

"You're welcome." I kissed her mouth hard as she sat on my lap. I hated seeing tears on her face. Our lips parted and I met her eyes, "I love you." I whispered.

"I love you too." Her hands rested on my shoulders, as I kissed her again.

I allowed my hands to travel up underneath her skirt, I was expecting to feel the silkiness of her panties, but they weren't there.

"Okay," she said, laughing as she grabbed my arm and pushed my hand away. "You need to behave." She giggled, sliding off my lap and adjusting her skirt.

"Are you not wearing any panties?" I questioned, my cock instantly growing hard at the thought. I remembered the last time that had happened. I'd ended up with her on the top of desk, legs spread, while I devoured her pussy until she screamed my name.

The light blush on her cheeks said it all, and my cock ached as she turned around, her perfect ass in my face as she adjusted and smoothed her skirt. She wasn't getting away from me. Instead, I grabbed her hips and stood up behind her, pulling her body against me.

"Spencer," She whispered, her voice cracking.

"Put your hands on my desk," I commanded in a hushed but firm tone. I didn't move while I waited for her to do what I said.

"Spencer, everyone is here. We can't do this now.,"

I leaned over her, bringing my lips to her ear. The smell of her, combined with the fact that I knew she wasn't wearing anything under that skirt, went straight to my cock. "Put your hands on my desk," I growled.

Her cheeks darkened as she did as I asked. I walked around to the door and turned the little lock I'd had installed after she'd started working here and turned back to see her standing there with her eyes closed. I smiled to myself and walked back around behind her. She sucked in a breath as I ran my hands up her sides, around to the front and held her full breasts in my hand, running my thumbs over her already hardened nipples.

"Remember what happened the last time you weren't wearing anything under your skirt?" I whispered.

"I do." She let out a breath as she pushed her chest into my hands. She was already breathing hard and I'd barely touched her. I kept one breast in my hand and reached down and pulled at her skirt, lifting it up over her ass. I ran my hand over her bare skin and reached around in front, my fingers finding that small bundle of nerves. She let out a soft moan as I kissed the back of her neck.

"Do you do this to me on purpose?" I questioned as I pressed up against her so she could feel my arousal.

"No." Her voice trembled as I continued gently rubbing her.

She was about to move her hands, but I shook my head. "Keep your hands there," I whispered. My cock strained against the fabric of my suit pants. I opened the zipper, allowing for some relief before continuing.

"Bend forward," I whispered, "and keep quiet."

She lowered herself down on the desk a little, and I gripped my cock, pulling it from my boxers and lining myself up with her opening. I slid myself into her and we both let out a moan. I could feel her tightening around me already as I thrust myself deeply into her again and again.

I reached around her, stroking that little bundle of nerves as I continued pumping into her. She grabbed my other hand, interlocking her fingers with mine. "Keep quiet," I whispered as I sucked her earlobe between my lips.

"Spencer."

"Shhh baby, just feel me, know how much I love you." I whispered, nipping at her neck.

"I'm gonna come," she cried a little louder than she should be.

"Shhh..." I pumped into her harder, working my hand faster between her legs. Her hand gripped mine tighter. I could feel her beginning to tighten and pulse around my cock, her once muted cries now audible as she let herself go. I took her mouth with mine, silencing her, as I pumped into her the last few times before I let go.

Both of us breathing hard, I held her in my arms as we both came down. Then I slipped myself from her and pulled her skirt down over her ass. She turned around and looked up at me, a satisfied yet tired look on her face. I zipped up my pants and then leaned onto my desk as I kissed her lips.

"You better fix your shirt and your hair," I whispered, nipping at her lower lip. "Don't want anyone to see how beautiful you are after I just fucked you." I winked.

Her cheeks went a deep pink again. "And you better tuck your shirt in," she answered back.

We both took a minute, adjusted our clothing so we looked suitable again. "So, you're taking the day off correct?" I questioned as I reached for my wallet that sat on the corner of my desk and flipped it open, pulling out my credit card.

"Ainsley?"

"Hmmm?" She looked up at me, then down at my hand.

"You're taking the rest of the day off. Go do some wedding things. Get your dress, have a massage. Enjoy your day."

She looked at me. "I thought you said we would do the dress thing together."

I shook my head. "It's bad luck, remember?"

"But I have work things to complete before I do any of that today," she argued, pushing my hand away.

"Yes, I know you do. However, most of those things can be done later tonight, from home. I want you to take the day." I walked around my desk and over to her. I slid the card into her hand and leaned in, taking her lips with mine. "Go, before you get me all worked up again. There is nothing more that I want to do than eat that sweet pussy for hours, but I need to concentrate," I said, gripping her ass and kissing her lips one more time.

She slipped the card from my hand and looked up at me. "Thank you," she whispered.

"I'll see you at home tonight. Drive careful."

Ainsley

"Ainsley and Carly." The barista called as she placed our coffee down on the counter.

I stopped talking as we both stepped forward and picked them up.

"Thank you," I called, waving to the girl as we made our way out the door and over to the only bridal shop in this shopping area. We stepped inside to be greeted by a sea of white dresses.

"This is a little overwhelming," I said, looking around, wondering where the hell to start.

"Do you have any idea what it is you're looking for?" Carly asked as we removed our shoes as the sign inside the door asked.

"I have a couple of ideas of what I want," I said, removing my jacket and hanging it up on the coat rack. "I found the perfect dress in a magazine. Trina told me they may have it here or at another store."

"Well, let's see if we can find it, shall we?" Carly said, taking a few steps into the shop.

"Oh, girls, no coffee on the floor." I turned in time to see a panicked woman who worked at the shop rushing toward us. "Welcome, ladies. Sorry, there is no coffee on the floor. Now, what can I help you with today?"

I let out a sigh and looked at Carly, who smiled smugly at me, then slipped my cup from my hand and took a seat on the couch just inside the door. "I'll just sit here. Go browse. See what she can help you with today."

I looked back at Carly and stifled a laugh as the woman pulled me toward a rack of dresses and began showing them to me one by one. By the time I got to the third rack, I was annoyed. This woman's attitude was the pits, and she was showing me everything I told her I didn't want. When I glanced over at Carly, I saw boredom lining her face as she flipped through her phone.

"Do you not like any of these, either?" the woman asked.

I shook my head. "No but thank you. I think I am just going to go somewhere else."

The woman gave me an irritated smile as I left her standing there and made my way back over to Carly, who stood up with an excited look on her face.

"Tired of Miss Stuck-up?" She giggled, handing me my coffee. "No coffee on the floor," Carly mimicked.

I laughed. "Yes, let's go somewhere else."

Within minutes, we were back in the car and headed to a shop that Trina had suggested. This time, we left our drinks in the car and headed inside to find a very relaxed atmosphere. A couple of groups of girls were there shopping as well, laughing and giggling at the dresses as they pulled them off the racks. I smiled at Carly, and together we made our way into the store. The first rack of dresses we came to I pulled out one dress and held it up. It was almost what I was looking for.

"Have you even set a date yet?" Carly asked as she pulled a dress off a rack and looked at it.

"No, not yet. We are still waiting to hear from the venues we contacted. We need to know what dates they have first. I think we sent requests to six places, and since it's such short notice, we kind of have to play by their rules."

"Okay then, let me rephrase my question. When are you trying to get married?"

I pulled out a dress and quickly changed my mind, then looked over at my best friend. "You know... in the next six weeks. For obvious reasons," I said, placing my hand on my belly.

Carly shoved the dress she'd been looking at back into the pile and turned to me with a frown on her face. "You mean in the next six weeks, so the pregnancy isn't obvious? Is that your idea or his?"

I immediately stopped looking at the dresses and turned to my best friend. "Why did you ask me like that?" I questioned.

"Like what?"

"If it were his idea or mine? You know, Spencer is a good man, despite what you and some others might think. I know you've had challenges with us, and I know you aren't his biggest fan, but I love him."

"I didn't mean it in any way, Ainsley. I guess I just meant it was a good reason. Was it your idea or his?" she said, changing the tone of her voice before turning back to the dresses in front of her. "Now, what do you think of this one?" she said, pulling out the next dress.

I just about screamed because it was the exact dress I'd bookmarked off the site. "Oh my God, that's it!" I cried, looking at the gorgeous white dress.

"What is it?"

"That's the dress!" I said, taking it from her and looking around for someone to allow me access to the changing room.

Half an hour later, I stood at the counter with Carly by my side as they completed the order for the dress. Lucky for me, they had one close to my size in stock, which made alterations much cheaper and easier. I paid for the dress and then we made our way to the car.

"When does the dress come in again?"

"Should be here by Friday," I sang. The feeling of removing one weight off my shoulders felt amazing.

"That's good."

"Yes, it will be perfect, since we do not know where the wedding is going to be held. That dress will work perfectly both at an inside and outside venue. I cannot wait for Spencer to see it!"

"Ainsley, you can't show Spencer!"

"Why not?"

"What do you mean? It's bad luck, like super bad luck. On second thought, you should wear it home. I'll wait for you here. Just take the one they have inside."

"Ugh, you aren't helping. Let's go." I giggled.

We'd just hopped on the freeway and began driving as Carly cracked open the bag of chips she purchased from the store before we left. "Want any?" she questioned.

"No, I'm good, thanks," I said, concentrating on the road in front of me. There was no way I could stuff my face with chips now that I needed to make sure I could fit into that wedding dress once the alterations were done.

"Oh, we should also work on the baby shower invites," Carly suggested.

"I wasn't planning on having a baby shower." I shrugged. "Besides, it's super early."

"There is no way on this planet that this baby will not get a shower from her Aunt Carly. I mean, just because I don't agree with your relationship decisions doesn't mean that a baby needs to be punished." She giggled. "We'll just invite a few people from school and our parents, of course."

"Okay." I sighed. "Whatever you say. When did you want to have that?"

"Oh, after the wedding, which was why I wanted to know the date, silly. I already bought the cards. I just need to let people know when to RSVP by."

"I don't know, let's do it in July. Pick a date."

"All right! July 15th. It's a Saturday," Carly answered as she checked the calendar on her phone. "I already sent you an invitation. It should go directly into your calendar."

"Perfect. Can't wait." I sighed, "When are you planning to send out the invites?" I questioned.

"Soon. I mean it will be in the middle of summer, so I'd like to give people the opportunity to go. You know, summer holidays and all."

"Whatever, do me one little favour please." I knew there was no way to stop her. Her mind was made up, the invites were going because she'd already decided that she was throwing me a shower.

"What is that?"

"Do not invite my father and Joan until after Spencer and I speak to them."

"I thought you guys spoke already. You said your father was down about getting married."

"Yes, we did. About the wedding, that is all," I muttered.

Carly stopped eating, and out of the corner of my eye, I knew she was staring at me. "You mean you didn't tell him everything?"

I shook my head. "No, we figured we'd drop that bomb after the wedding. Besides, it's so early. We really shouldn't be telling anyone."

"Ainsley, why?" Carly cried. "Why are you being this way? It's your father."

"I'm being that way because it's too early. I haven't even had my appointment with this OB/GYN my doctor is referring me to. So please, do as I ask." I could feel myself on the verge of tears as I looked at my best friend.

"Okay, okay," Carly said, shoving her hand back into the bag of chips.

Spencer

One week later

It was already after six when I made my way across the parking lot to my car. I shoved my laptop bag and the pile of reports I still needed to go over in the back seat and climbed in, starting the engine. I was about to back out of the spot when my phone vibrated. I pulled it from my breast pocket to see that my brother Max had texted. Instead of responding, I dialed his number and waited while his voice came over the line.

"You got my email?" Max questioned.

"I did. Haven't looked at the attachment yet. I'm just on my way home."

"Gotcha. Well, first I'd like to say that I'm sorry I couldn't make it to the engagement thing. You know how it is."

I let out a breath. "No, Max, I don't know how it is."

"Well, you know, things just sort of crept up." He chuckled.

I frowned. "Things sort of crept up?" I repeated. "Let me guess, a woman?"

I knew my brother well—too well, to be honest.

"Yeah, and the situation, it was, shall we say, unavoidable? Besides, it was only an engagement party. It's not like it was an enormous deal, like the wedding."

This was Max. However, it was a big deal. It was a big deal to both Ainsley and me. I cleared my throat and thought a moment before speaking. "Max, you know, the least you could do is show a little support. Especially since I just handed you an enormous opportunity, basically on a silver platter. I gave you the reins to oversee the Denver office, when it should have gone to one of my senior executives working right under me. I pride myself on promoting and hiring from within first. Instead, I somehow took pity on my brother, who's fucked up more than the average person, only to have him spit in my face."

"Come on, Spencer, I didn't spit in your face." Max huffed.

"Whatever, Max. You didn't even send back the RSVP." I didn't really have the energy to deal with this phone call right now. I was tired and hungry and still had a few hours of work to complete before the meeting tomorrow morning. "Listen, I'll call you in the morning. Be prepared to go over all your opening numbers tomorrow on the call."

"Tomorrow?" Max questioned.

I was silent for a moment as I stopped at the traffic light. I ran my hand over my face. "Yes, Max, tomorrow's meeting. Nine, does it sound familiar?"

"Yeah, yep, I'll talk to you then."

I hung up the phone and turned up the radio just as my phone rang again.

"Hey, Spencer!" Nick's voice came over the line.

"Hey, Nick! Any news?"

"They accepted the offer. We set the closing date as you asked. I also have a few appointments lined up to show your place. Honestly, it should sell fast. I've had lots of interest so far."

"Perfect, thanks, Nick. Whatever needs to be signed, just fax it to my home office. Also, can you send me the dates you need to show our place? I want to make sure we have everything in place."

"Can do. Talk to you soon."

I hopped on the highway, turned the radio up, and made my way home. Twenty minutes later, I pulled into our driveway, gathered my items from the back seat, and headed to the door. I'd just slid my key in the lock and opened the door to be greeted by Carly walking behind Nikki.

"Daddy!" Nikki cried.

"Shhh... Ainsley is sleeping, remember?" Carly whispered. "Take your crayons and colouring book into the kitchen."

Nikki looked at me and then hung her head and stomped into the kitchen. "Why is Ainsley asleep?" I asked, dropping my stuff inside the door, and heading up the stairs, glancing in the living room to see Ainsley sound asleep under a blanket on the couch.

"She just passed out on the couch. We were sitting talking about the baby shower. I was telling her I'd mailed out all the invitations, and when I looked over, she was out." Carly shrugged.

"Is she all right?" I asked, taking another look at Ainsley. "Baby shower?" I questioned when I realized what she'd said.

"Yes, baby shower. I planned one for her."

"I see," I said, looking at Ainsley. "Don't you think it's a little early to be inviting people to a baby shower?"

"God, you sound just like Ainsley." Carly shrugged.

"Yes, we haven't even seen the OB/GYN yet, and besides, we aren't even married yet!"

"Yes, but we aren't having the baby shower until July, and I wanted to make sure people save the date."

I rolled my eyes. "Who did you invite?"

"Don't worry. I will tell you who I didn't invite, and that is Ainsley's father and Jane."

"For the love of God." I breathed under my breath, praying that she was only joking with me now. "I'm concerned," I said.

"Why?"

"It's not like her to sleep in the middle of the day. Was she feeling okay?"

"She was feeling fine when we returned today. However, if you wake her, I will hurt you. Got it, Big Guy? She probably just needs some rest."

"Yeah, I got it, but is she okay?" I questioned again, worried that perhaps something happened today to make her not feel well. I knew that her and Ainsley were going to the bridal shop again for sizing and to pick out a bridesmaid dress for Carly. Maybe it was all the baby shower talk, or that Carly had apparently sent out invites. Then there was the thought that perhaps she had run into Brittany again.

"My God, what do you mean is she okay? You knocked her up! She may be twenty, but it seems your baby is sucking the life out of my best friend. Also, be forewarned, you may have ruined that body forever!"

I rolled my eyes and let out a sigh. "Yes, I knocked her up, fine. However, women give birth every day, Carly. Her body will not be ruined."

Carly shrugged. "All I'm saying is I hope you aren't too attached to it."

"For the love of God, Carly. You do realize that I am in love with the person, not the body. The body is just a bonus. It's not a requirement."

"Huh?"

I looked at the shock on Carly's face and smiled inwardly at myself. "Exactly what I said. The body is a bonus, not a requirement. I'm in love with Ainsley."

Carly was quiet for a moment as she stared at me. "God... make me want to puke."

I smirked to myself as she turned her back to me and slipped her feet into her shoes. "I'm going home now, before you begin growing on me. Can't have that happening or the next thing I know I'll be rooting for the pair of you."

Just then, Nikki appeared in the kitchen doorway and attached herself to my leg. "That's probably a good plan," I said.

"Just don't you wake her up. I'll keep you guys updated as to the RSVPs for the baby shower."

"Great." I chuckled to myself as she pulled the door open. "Good night, Carly. See you soon." As much as she annoyed me, she was growing on me. However, I was concerned with the slew of phone calls Ainsley may get once her friends began getting invites to a baby shower.

When the door clicked shut, I turned to Nikki. "She is

crazy," I said, crossing my eyes and sticking out my tongue. Nikki burst into a fit of giggles.

"What do you say you help me with dinner? We have a surprise for Ainsley," I whispered.

"We do? What is it?" she whispered, her eyes growing wide.

"It's a surprise for you too. Now come into the kitchen and we will quietly get things ready. Plus, you can help me put this up," I said, producing a package containing a banner.

Nikki jumped up and down and then turned and ran into the kitchen while I followed behind her.

Ainsley

I woke up to the sound of music and Spencer's voice in the kitchen, then the aroma of garlic bread hit my nose, making my stomach growl. I looked at my phone to see it was almost eight. I must have fallen asleep, I thought to myself as I kicked the blanket off me. I got up off the couch, stretched, and made my way into the kitchen. Nikki was sitting on the counter, helping Spencer. "Okay, sprinkle the cheese into the pot," he said.

I smiled, watching the two of them. Nikki let out a little laugh as she sprinkled cheese into the pot.

"Sorry, I must have drifted off," I said.

Spencer turned and smiled in my direction, while Nikki added in another handful of cheese into the pot he was stirring. "All right, miss, that is enough cheese." He chuckled, putting the pot to the back of the stove and grabbing Nikki, placing her down on the floor.

"Don't look behind you, Ainsley." Nikki giggled, covering her mouth with her hands.

"Why not? What's behind me?" I questioned.

Spencer walked over and pulled me into his arms, kissing my cheek. "A surprise," he whispered.

"Can she see now, Daddy?" Nikki cried. "Please."

Spencer looked from me down to Nikki and let out a sigh. "Well, I guess," he said, turning me around.

I looked up to see a banner on the wall that read 'Congratulations on your New Home!"

I couldn't help but stare at the words on the sign. Thoughts of us owning our own place, the one we chose together, brought tears to my eyes. I was so excited. I could feel Spencer watching me, and I quickly wiped away the tear that sat at the corner of my eye before it slid down my cheek.

"You happy?" Spencer questioned.

I nodded my head. "Yes, very much so. I'm very excited," I said, throwing my arms around his neck and hugging him.

"As am I. Now we should eat," he said, meeting my lips. "I'm sure you're starved."

I nodded, wrapping my arm around Nikki as she hugged my leg. I'd just gotten her settled in her chair when I remembered I still had Spencer's credit card in my purse from a week ago. I reached for my bag that sat on the counter and opened my wallet, taking the card out.

"Before I forget," I said, holding the card out for him to take. "I should have given this back to you last week. I totally forgot."

He shook his head, his hands full. "Keep it. Honestly, you are going to need it for the wedding, especially if I am in a meeting. Plus, we now have a house to furnish." He winked. "I'll see about ordering you a spousal card as well. But for now, use it at your leisure."

I softly smiled and slid the card back into my wallet, then took the salad from Spencer and put it on the table while he brought over the pasta and garlic bread.

"How did the dress fitting go?" Spencer questioned as he began plating dinner.

"Good, just a few minor alterations." I smiled. "I go back for another one in a couple of weeks. I can't wait for you to see it."

"I want to see it too!" Nikki said.

"Of course you'll see it, probably before Daddy." I winked. "Especially since you are going to need a flower girl dress," I said, tickling her tummy.

She let out a loud giggle. "Really?"

"Yes, really." I winked.

"Carly told me she is planning a baby shower."

"Yes, she sort of took that upon herself. I tried to tell

her it was too early, but she insisted on sending out the invites."

"Yes, she seemed proud of herself as well. Has anyone messaged you yet?"

"No. I'm afraid of that starting though." I shrugged. "It's too early to tell people."

"Agreed."

"Invites are out, though, so I'm not sure what I am supposed to do." I shrugged, pinching the bridge of my nose to try and stop the headache that was coming. "Guess I'll just cross that bridge when I come to it."

We all sat down to eat. The conversation during dinner was about the house. Nikki was excited that she was going to have a bigger room, and when she found out that there was a pool in the backyard, all she wanted to do was get into her suit and go swimming, which caused Spencer and I both to laugh.

Once dinner was over, I gave Nikki a bath and got her tucked into bed while Spencer went over some reports, then I too got into my pajamas. I took a few minutes and cleaned up the kitchen while I made a cup of tea and then settled into the living room, resting my head as my favourite jazz album played over the stereo. My dad would be returning from his trip with Jane tonight. I was excited to see him in the morning.

I looked down at my hands while sitting on the couch and noticed my fingers were swollen. I pulled at my engagement ring, finally feeling it slip from my finger, and set it on the side table. Spencer and I had talked about when to tell him about the baby. We'd agreed to do it before the wedding, and we figured that once they returned from their trip, and we'd seen the OB/GYN, we'd tell them. That way, Jane could help with Carly's baby shower.

Spencer came upstairs and glanced in the living room at me. "I'm just gonna grab a coffee. I fear it's going to be a late night for me," he sighed. "I still have a lot of things to go over."

"I'd offer to help, but I'm exhausted, so I'll probably crawl into bed soon," I replied, getting up and following him into the kitchen where I ran my swollen hands under water and dried them. "I hate going to bed alone," I said, wrapping my arms around his waist and pressing my body into his back. My hands traveled down to his hips, and I was just about to run my hand over the bulge I already knew was growing when the doorbell rang.

"I'll get it," I said, releasing my hold on him.

"Just check who it is first," he cautioned.

"I will." I walked to the door and glanced out the side window to see my father standing there. I pulled the door open and opened my arms, expecting a hug. Instead, he pushed past me and stormed into the house, shutting the door behind him.

"Where is he?" he demanded. "I think I might kill him this time."

The crazed look on his face scared me. "Dad, what is it? What's wrong?" I questioned, my heart beating hard in my chest. I looked down at his hand to see a torn, open envelope.

My stomach churned at the thought of what that envelope contained, and I silently hoped it wasn't the invitation to the baby shower.

"Ainsley, what is it?" Spencer demanded, coming out of the kitchen, alarm in his voice.

"I really hope this is some kind of sick joke." My father's voice boomed throughout the entryway as he threw down the envelope he'd been carrying. I instantly recognized it as the envelope that had contained the baby shower invitation.

Carly had promised me she wouldn't give Dad his until later. Why would she have done this I wondered and then it hit, I'd sent her with some mail we'd had for him, and maybe it was accidentally put in his mailbox along with the other envelopes.

"Jon, just come in and we will talk this through," Spencer said, trying to calm my father down.

"How dare you? Is this what this wedding is about?" my father demanded.

"Jon, please, let's just talk about this like grown adults," Spencer repeated, keeping his voice at a level tone.

My dad glared at Spencer and then looked at me, disappointment flooding his face. Then he climbed up the stairs and followed Spencer into the kitchen. I'd just stepped into the kitchen while Spencer was getting ready to pour a coffee for my father when I remembered I hadn't ripped down the banner Spencer and Nikki had made. I did my best to grab my father's attention, but he'd already seen the banner, his face growing serious and angry.

"What the hell is that?" he questioned, looking toward the banner.

Immediately, I looked at Spencer, and I covered my mouth to keep the sobs from starting. Spencer gently shook his head, telling me not to say anything as he approached the table.

"Jon, we need to talk," he said.

"No shit, we need to talk. I agreed to you guys dating, and now marriage. However, I feel like you both have blindsided me once again. Now a baby and then this?" he said, pointing to the colourful banner that only a couple of hours ago had brought me joy.

"Daddy, please..."

"Don't Daddy me," my father said, turning his glaring eyes on me.

"Spencer is a good man." I cried.

Spencer reached for me and pulled me in behind him, protecting me from a man I'd known my entire life.

"He wants to marry you for all the wrong reasons,

Ainsley. He knows I'd kill him if he impregnated you and then left you to raise that baby all on your own. Isn't that right, Spencer?" my father screamed.

"That is true, Jon. You would kill me. However, that isn't what this is. I'm in love with her. Yes, she is pregnant, and yes, we are getting married, but I planned to ask her to marry me before I even knew about the baby. We bought a house, one we can call our own, but not one of these things has anything to do with one another."

"How would I know that? There seems to be no truth to any of this!" my father shouted. "You know, this is all just going way too fast. Young lady, you need to move back home this minute. I will not allow you to ruin your life. Now go get your things."

My throat got tight, and tears streamed down my face. I was finding it hard to breathe and began panicking at the thought of losing Spencer and Nikki again. I grabbed hold of Spencer's arm as I fought to control the panic I was feeling. Dizziness was setting in.

"Stop it, Ainsley. I will not allow you to move away with this man. I should have stuck to my decision last year. I should have forced you to quit your job. I'm guessing the flu was really morning sickness! I knew I should have immediately made you see the doctor. I never dreamed..."

"Jon, please... just calm down," Spencer commanded as he wrapped his arm around me, trying to get me to calm down. "Ainsley, breathe, baby," he said in a low voice.

Only I couldn't. My chest was so tight I couldn't inhale. The thought of losing Spencer, Nikki, or my father was too much for me to handle as tears streamed freely down my face. Spencer wrapped his arms around me, holding me as I sobbed.

"You know, when I told you to find a younger woman to help you get over Brittany, I honestly never thought it would be my daughter you'd turn to. Sneaking around behind my back. I tried hard to be rational and allow you two to date. I even swallowed my fears of what your intentions were with the proposal, but to find all this out now, I have nothing left to say. I want you home!"

"I was going to talk to you. You shouldn't even have gotten one of those invites until after we spoke."

"When were you planning on talking to me, after the fucking wedding?" my father yelled and stepped forward, taking hold of my upper arm.

Immediately, Spencer grabbed his arm, forcing him to remove his hand from me and stepped in front of me. "Jon, I'm warning you. Don't touch her. Now, I never meant for this to happen this way. I never meant to fall in love with your daughter, but I have zero fucking regrets. Now I will not tell you again. You either calm down and talk to us or you leave our home. This isn't good for Ainsley or the baby."

As the words left Spencer's lips, my heart began

racing. At first, I thought maybe my father hadn't heard him, but he stopped moving and stood there, staring at us.

"Tell me I didn't actually hear what I think you said," my father said in a low, controlled voice.

"No, you heard me correctly." Spencer stood there, his back straight, his eyes glued to my father's. He wasn't backing down, not this time. I turned my back away from the two of them, afraid of what was coming next. I left the kitchen, stepping into the living room and up against the wall as the room I'd just left fell completely silent.

I tried to breathe, tried to calm down, but the room spun. Still, there were no words spoken between the two of them. The kitchen was completely silent. I wanted them to yell at one another, to get it over with so we could sit down and talk things through after, like rational adults. Instead, the silence was overwhelming, until I heard my father speak.

"Fine, kick me out. She can stay here tonight, but I want her home in the fucking morning. Got it." The front door opened and then closed. Then, suddenly, Spencer appeared beside me.

"He left?" I questioned, looking at Spencer with tear filled eyes.

Spencer nodded his head. "He did."

Tears poured. "Just like that, he left?"

Spencer grabbed me, pulling me into him, doing his

best to comfort me. "It's okay, Ainsley, shhh. I promise things will be fine. I'll speak to him tomorrow."

"I'm not going there." I sobbed. "I'm not leaving us."

"You don't have to." Spencer's arms tightened around me, and I cried harder. I was afraid that with all this backlash that Spencer would soon tire of being the one to hold us together and that he too would give up on us. After all, he didn't need this type of drama in his life.

"Come, we are getting you into bed," he whispered, grabbing the remote for the stereo and silencing the music I'd been enjoying before all the craziness had erupted. He turned out all the lights, then quickly locked the front door and walked with me into the bedroom.

I pulled back the blankets and crawled into bed as tears still ran down my cheeks. My body was exhausted, and as soon as my head hit the pillow, I let out a yawn. He turned his bedside lamp on and then shut off the overhead light, coming around to his side of the bed. He stripped down and slipped under the covers, his warm body sliding behind me, providing me with comfort, while I shivered.

He pulled me into him, my head resting on his shoulder, and wrapped his arm around me. Not another word spoken between us. He just held me tightly against him. I never wanted to leave his arms. I closed my eyes and took comfort in the security and warmth he provided, finally drifting off into a restless sleep.

Spencer

It had been four days since the confrontation with Ainsley's father.

Ainsley had asked me repeatedly when I planned to speak to Jon. I could see the stress piled not only on her face, but in her actions and body language. However, I took it upon myself to decide it was just best to let things calm down before I tried to speak with him. I wanted things to be as stressless for Ainsley as possible, and I figured letting him calm down first would help the situation and make him more receptive to hearing me out.

Even though I knew this, I was still worried about her. She hadn't been feeling well the last few days, and I was concerned for not only her wellbeing but that of the baby too. I feared if Jon wasn't receptive to talking this through, our situation would become worse, and that would only upset Ainsley more, which was the last thing I wanted.

I got up from my chair and walked over to my printer when my office door opened and Ainsley appeared. "I made myself a tea, thought I'd bring you a coffee," she said, placing the mug down on my desk. She didn't make any eye contact with me, instead, she walked over to the window, looking thoughtfully at the city beyond and saying nothing.

I frowned. "How are you feeling?"

She looked at me over her shoulder. I tried to hide the worry from my face, but I knew she could see it. She turned and went back to silently looking out the window.

"Ainsley, how are you feeling?" I repeated.

"Okay," she answered, then she began quietly humming a song to herself as she looked back out the window. I guessed she was only trying to wash away my fears, but I also knew by the look on her face, and this odd behavior that she wasn't telling me the truth.

"You're sure?" I questioned.

She nodded. "I sent through the reports from Max," she said, picking up a sliver of paper off the floor. "Did you get them?"

I nodded. "I did. I'll be going over them shortly. When do you have your next visit with the doctor?"

"My family doctor booked me in with an OB/GYN. I'm just waiting for the appointment date." She walked over to me and placed her hand on my chest and looked me in the eye. "Please, Spencer, I'm okay. I'll order you some lunch. What would you like?"

"Just order from the same place you are ordering from for yourself." She didn't respond. She just walked over and looked out the window again. "Ainsley, did you hear me?"

"No, I'm sorry."

"I told you to order me whatever you were having. Now I know you heard me." I frowned.

"Oh, sorry, I'm not eating today. I'm not really all that hungry," she muttered.

As it was, Ainsley ate like a bird. Her family doctor had told her she needed to make sure she was getting enough at the very first appointment when they'd gone over her diet. There was no way she wasn't eating. She'd barely touched dinner last night, and I was sure she'd thrown her breakfast in the garbage this morning, after I'd told her I may need to make a trip to Denver.

I cleared my throat. "Don't order me anything. We are going out for lunch," I said, putting an end to what I feared would become an argument. "Be ready for one, right after my meeting." I glanced at my calendar, making sure I had nothing booked until at least three.

"Fine," Ainsley huffed. She made her way to the door and stepped out into the hallway, pulling the door closed behind her.

My meeting made my head ache. I'd gone over all the

documents with Max over the phone again and to say they did not impress me was an understatement. I was glad I'd decided to take Ainsley for lunch; I needed to get out of this office to clear my head.

I glanced at my watch and grabbed my suit jacket off the back of my chair. I stepped out into the hallway and saw that Ainsley had stepped away from her desk. I was about to text her when she came walking around the corner, holding her stomach.

"You feeling okay?"

"Yep, of course. Just a little upset stomach is all."

"It's because you haven't eaten. Let's go."

"I've eaten, Spencer," Ainsley bit back.

It was out of character for her to snap back at me. I ignored it. "Ainsley, half an egg does not count as eating." I walked over and grabbed her coat from the rack in the corner and helped her into it, and then I grabbed her hand and guided her to the elevator where we both stood in silence, waiting.

Once at the restaurant, Ainsley sat with the menu open in front of her, trying to decide what it was she wanted to eat. I'd decided ten minutes earlier, and I glanced at my watch as she continued to go back and forth between the three dishes.

"Okay, I think I've got it," she said, closing the menu.

Immediately, I signaled for the server. Once we'd ordered, I sat back in my chair and looked at Ainsley.

"How did the meeting with Max go?" she questioned.

I knew she was trying to avoid me asking her anything, which was fine for now.

I cleared my throat. "Well, I am not pleased. I am going to need to make a trip out there for a few days. Max has never overseen something this large before, and to save a disaster, I'd rather take control and set things right at the beginning, as opposed to waiting."

Ainsley nodded her head and muttered, "That's understandable," then looked away from me. "I know how hard you've worked to get Denver up and running."

"Would you be willing to stay with Nikki at the house for a few days while I go?"

When she didn't immediately respond, I leaned forward. "Ainsley? What is it? Talk to me, please."

Her chest heaved as she took in a full breath. Avoiding my eyes, she shrugged. "Are you sure you're not running away from things here... from me?" Her voice cracked as she choked out the last two words.

"From you? Why would I be running from you?"

"Oh, I don't know, because of everything that has been going on in our lives as of late. I am sure you're growing tired of everything with my dad, the wedding, Brittany, the new baby, the new house, and probably a million other things I forgot to add to that list. I don't doubt that you'd be looking for space," she said as she counted items on her fingers. "Oh, and don't forget the baby shower invites."

I frowned. "No, Ainsley, this isn't about needing space. This is about business. While all of those things are going on, and yes, it can be stressful, you need to keep yourself focused on the end goal. That goal is us and our family."

"I know. It just feels like all we are doing is treading through rough waters, and it's been that way since all this started. It's literally killing me that the two most important people in my life are showing me zero support."

"Your father will come around. That I can promise you. I assume Carly would be the other one."

Ainsley nodded. "Yes."

"She is throwing you a baby shower. Doesn't that count as showing you support?"

"Sure, but it's a baby shower I asked her to wait for. Other than that, her entire focus has been coming up with reasons I should just find someone else."

"Well, all I can say is that she will understand much better when she meets someone."

"I never looked at it that way. She hasn't ever been in a relationship. She has no idea how I feel about you."

"Exactly. When it's true love, nothing should stand in the way of it. No matter what anyone says. Deep down, I know Carly is there for you. She puts on a good game, but you mean a lot to her. I can see that, otherwise she wouldn't be there every time you need her. I also know you mean the world to your father, so please never think for a moment he'd disown you. I know how that man feels about you. If he didn't care, he wouldn't fly off the handle every time. He's just having a hard time accepting what is happening, but eventually he is going to have to accept it. He will come around."

Ainsley nodded. I watched as her eyes fell to her hands. I cleared my throat. "Look at me." I waited until she lifted her head and her eyes met mine. "I meant what I said the other night. I regret nothing about us. You need to know that. But you also need to ask yourself the question, is this what you really want?"

"What do you mean?"

"Do you really want us?" I replied, praying, and hoping she said yes, because I didn't know what I would do if she said no. I'd grown to love her more than anyone I'd ever been with. She meant the world to me, and I had vowed to myself that I would fight to keep her, no matter what, because my world would shatter the day she ever walked out of my life.

"I do, but I also want everyone else to be happy for us, too."

"Well, love, that is impossible. There will always be someone who doesn't approve of every relationship, especially ours. What matters is that you and I are happy. That is it. That's all that matters."

Her eyes met mine, and she sat there for a minute saying nothing, then she softly smiled. "I want this. I want us so badly. Those few weeks we were apart were hell for me. I never want to feel that way again."

"I feel the same way. Without you was hell. So how about we focus on us and put a lot of this noise behind us? Everything will work out," I said, taking her hand in mine.

"Thank you for being here. I love you."

"I love you, Ainsley. I'll always be here for you, for whatever you need. Now let's get back on track and focus on my question..."

"Of course, I'll stay with Nikki."

"Good. I thought you could work from home and possibly take her shopping for some things for the new house. She was showing me some new bedding she'd like. I told her to put it on her Christmas list, but I don't see any reason to make her wait."

"Yes, I could also begin packing, too."

I shook my head. "No, I am hiring a company to do that. They will begin after I am back. Now what you can do is call those venues we contacted and find out what ones are available."

"I can do that," she said with a smile.

"Good, and after lunch, can you also book my flight?"

"Yes, of course. I'll do it as soon as we get back to the office."

"Perfect. Now let's enjoy this beautiful day and our lunch."

Ainsley

Spencer was leaving for Denver. I'd gotten him an early-morning flight and booked his hotel for three nights. Nikki and I drove Spencer to the airport, and we sat in the car watching as he headed to the front doors with his luggage.

"Bye, Daddy!" Nikki yelled from the backseat window.

Spencer turned around and waved at us. "See you soon," he called.

We watched until he'd gone through the doors, then I hit the button to roll up the windows and turned on some music. I hadn't told Nikki that she wasn't going to school today. Instead, I figured I'd surprise her when I pulled into the mall parking lot.

"Ainsley, am I going to be late for school?" Nikki asked from the backseat.

"No, babe, you're not. We are on our way right now," I said, glancing in the driver's side mirror to make sure the lane was clear before I pulled away from the curb.

"Ainsley, did Daddy tell you I want a pink blanket for my new room?"

"He did. He even showed me the picture you showed him. It's really pretty."

"Do you think you could get it for me? Then I could be like my friend Haley, who lives across the street. She has one just like it, and I just love it so much."

I did my best to keep a straight face. "Well, what did your dad say? Did you ask him?"

"He told me to put it on my Christmas list, but I know that if you got it for me, he wouldn't be angry."

I smiled. "Well, I don't know. I think maybe I should talk to him about it first," I said and glanced in the rearview mirror just in time to see her pout.

"Okay," she said, letting out a huff and crossing her arms in front of her chest.

I did my best not to laugh at her actions as I drove down the freeway and pulled off at the exit for the mall, coming to a stop at the lights before turning into the large parking lot. I drove around, finally finding a spot, and shut the car off.

"Where are we?" Nikki asked, looking out the back window. "This doesn't look like school."

"It's not. We are at the mall. You and I are spending the day together. We are going to get some things for your room at the new house," I said, climbing out of the car and opening the back door.

"Yay! Can we get my blanket, please, Ainsley? I promise I will be a good girl."

"Well, I wanted it to be a surprise, but yes, we can," I said, kissing her forehead as I helped her out of the back of the car.

Nikki pulled on my arm as we headed into the mall, excited to get her blanket. I wasted no time. We made our way into the bedding store and right over to the kids' section. Within minutes, she'd found the same one her friend had, and she also found three others she liked. Now we stood before four sets of bedding, two of them pink, and two light purple.

I watched as Nikki walked around each bag, looking at each one repeatedly. I glanced at my watch. We'd been standing here for the past twenty-five minutes.

"I just don't know, Ainsley. I love this one..." she said, hugging the bag that contained the original blanket, "but I like the others too."

"Well, sweets, you need to decide. You really seemed to have your heart set on the first one. I say we go with it, and perhaps we could also get you a new sheet set, only get that in purple. That way, you have a little of both colours," I said, reaching up and pulling a set of purple sheets down from the shelf.

"Ohhh, I like that idea!"

"All right then. You take these sheets, and I will carry the bedding," I said, winking at her, while I put the three other comforters back on the shelf.

I grabbed her hand, and we began walking toward the cashier when Nikki spotted a pink pillow. "Can I get this too?" she asked, letting go of my hand as we walked by to grab the heart-shaped pillow.

I took one look at her face. Her eyes said it all as she held the pillow to her chest. "Okay, fine." I winked again.

We headed to the cashier where I paid for the bedding, then we took it all out to the car before continuing through the mall. Nikki walked beside me, talking a mile a minute about how excited she was to use her new bedding, and I had to remind her many times that she had to wait until we moved.

We walked the mall the rest of the morning, stopping at some of Nikki's favourite stores. She showed me all the things she was going to put on her birthday list. She wanted me to make sure I knew what each item was because, according to her, Spencer had gotten the items wrong last year. I couldn't help but laugh at her serious-ness as I took a picture of a few toys she said she just had to have.

After lunch, we made our way back to the car. I now had a long list of items Nikki wanted for her birthday, and for Christmas. I pulled out of the parking lot and turned left, heading toward the bookstore.

"Can we get one of those special drinks at the bookstore?" Nikki asked as we made our way inside.

"What special drink would that be?" I asked, knowing full well she wanted a vanilla frappe.

"You know, one of those whipped-up drinks you bring home when you come here."

"Ohhh, one of those. I think we can." I giggled, pulling her close to me.

We stood in line, and when it was our turn, I stepped up to the counter and waited to place our order. Nikki pulled on my arm, wanting to show me something, and that was when I heard her voice.

"What can I get for you?"

I didn't want to turn around. I wanted to grab Nikki and run, only it was too late. She'd already seen us.

"Well, well, well, if it isn't the babysitter." Brittany stood behind the counter staring at me, and then she noticed Nikki. "Why the hell isn't Nikki in school?"

"Don't worry, her father knows. Actually, allowing her out of school for the day was his idea. Now, we'd like two vanilla Frappuccinos please."

She punched a couple of keys on the register with attitude and then looked at me. "Loading my child up on sugar, huh? Not a wonder why she always acts like a little brat when she's home."

"I highly doubt that I'm the problem."

"Oh, my dear, how naïve are you? You are the only problem that I see here. If you honestly think that by you ordering I am just going to drop the subject, you're more naïve than I thought."

Ignoring her, I pulled Spencer's card out of my wallet and handed it to her without thinking. I didn't understand what her problem was. All I knew was that I wanted this confrontation to end and for us to be away from her.

She looked down at the card and then up at me and chuckled to herself, shaking her head. "Living the high life, are you? You're living with him, fucking him, and also getting a paycheck from him. Why do you need his credit card, too?"

I felt my cheeks heat at her words.

"Oh wait, I know why. I mean, he was a mediocre fuck. He can only make up for it by padding your chequebook."

I was about to lean over the counter and tell Brittany to fuck herself when I heard Nikki call out to her. "Mommy, oh Mommy, just wait till you see what Ainsley got me."

Brittany looked at me and rolled her eyes.

"She got me a pretty pink blanket for our new house!" Nikki cried with excitement.

Brittany completely ignored her and continued to glare at me.

"Nikki, not now," I whispered as Brittany looked down at her. Once her eyes were off me, I closed my eyes and took in a breath. I just wanted out of here because I knew from here on things would not go over well.

"Is that so? Did you put it in on this card too? Perhaps I should call him and let him know I found his credit card, that some tramp stole it," she whispered as she leaned over the counter.

I glared at her. "Brittany, you really should calm down before you get fired from yet another job."

Brittany glared back at me and yelled out for two vanilla Frappuccinos. She ran Spencer's credit card through the machine and handed it back to me. Then, in a huff, she disappeared behind the counter, saying nothing to Nikki, who looked up at me with tears in her eyes.

"Did I do something wrong, Ainsley?" Nikki asked me, a tear slipping down her cheek.

"No, sweetie, you did nothing wrong. It appears your mother is having a bad day."

I occupied Nikki while we waited for our drinks, and I prayed Brittany didn't return to the counter. Once I heard my name called, we took our drinks and made our way into the bookstore, where we headed into the children's section to pick out a couple of new books for Nikki, when all I really wanted to do was go back home.

It was almost nine thirty by the time I crawled into bed. I'd put Nikki to bed at seven and read to her until she drifted off to sleep, then I sat down and caught up on work emails before taking a hot bath.

I then crawled into bed and snuggled down under the covers and turned on the TV. I searched until I found a show I'd been watching and then grabbed my phone to text Spencer. It was a pleasant surprise to find a message waiting for me instead.

> RomanticAlpha42: I'm at the hotel.
> Call me.

I dialled his number and waited for him to pick up. "Hey, sweetie."

"Hey, how did things go today?" his tired voice asked.

"Okay. We picked out her bedding for her room."

"Good. Was she happy?"

"She was so excited. I wish you could have seen her face. I also have a wish list of items for her birthday and for Christmas."

"I see." Spencer chuckled. "Everything else go okay?"

"Yeah, I ordered pizza for dinner. After spending the

day shopping and getting her bathed and ready for school tomorrow, I was exhausted."

"That's good. I am sure she enjoyed that."

"Yes, she did." I bit my bottom lip. I swallowed hard. I knew I had to tell Spencer about running into Brittany. What I didn't want was her calling him and lying about things at the bookstore today. For all I knew, she would turn the whole incident around on me.

"What else did you do?"

"We went to the bookstore." I grew quiet for a moment and took in a breath, "Oh, and we ran into Brittany today."

"What? Where?"

"At the bookstore. Well, actually, at the coffee shop. Nikki wanted a Frappuccino, so we went into the coffee house there. Brittany apparently works there now."

"And..."

"Oh, and she was her usual charming self."

"Did she take a tone with you?"

"She was worse there to me than she was the night at the restaurant. However, it's not me I'm worried about. It's how she treated Nikki."

"What the hell did she do?"

"Ignored her. Completely ignored her. I'm wondering if the acting out isn't from that."

Spencer was quiet for a few moments. "Perhaps I'll make a call to my lawyer, you know, and add more to the custody case. She always wanted to fight me on this. What else did she say?"

"Well, it made her angry Nikki wasn't in school. Then, without thinking, I gave her your credit card to pay for the drinks. She said she was going to call you."

"Did you tell her to go ahead?" he questioned.

"No, Spencer, I just wanted to be done with her."

"Are you sure you're okay on your own there? I hate you being alone."

"Spencer, please, don't worry about me. Nikki is fine, I am fine. Also, remember, my father, who still isn't speaking to me, is right next door. I know he would let nothing happen to us. I know he knows you're away because I saw him watching Nikki and I through his front window when we were getting out of the car. He also kept coming to his kitchen window when we were in the back-yard after dinner."

"I know. It's not the point. I should have brought you guys. It's not too late. You can book a flight, and I will have you picked up at the airport."

"Seriously, Spencer, we are fine. Carly is going to come over and spend the night tomorrow. If Brittany wants to stop by, she can deal with Carly." I giggled.

The line went quiet for a moment, then I heard Spencer clear his throat. "Perhaps alone may be better. Is she still all for team breakup?"

"Probably. Who knows with her? Last I spoke to her,

she told me she needed to limit the time she spent when you were around because you were growing on her. I don't even know what that means."

Spencer laughed. "I see. Perhaps I'll be in her good books one day after all."

"Did you speak to Max yet?"

"No, he doesn't even know I'm in town. I wanted to get settled in. The flight was late, so I decided I'd pop into the office tomorrow morning instead. I'll know more about what is going on after that meeting. I think I am going to treat him to dinner, just two brothers."

"That's good," I said, yawning.

"You in bed already?" Spencer questioned.

"Yeah, what about you?"

"No. I'm still working. I went over a lot of stuff on the flight, but I wanted to prepare a plan for Max. You know, goals. So that is what I'll be working on tonight."

"Yes, you had mentioned that you were going to work on that."

The line grew quiet, neither of us saying anything. As I lay there listening to him breathe, I wished Spencer were here beside me, holding me instead of being so far away.

"What are you thinking?" he asked, his voice low.

I didn't want to make him feel worse than he already did. I knew he didn't enjoy being away from us, and this time he was worried about us being alone, but I couldn't help wanting to be with him.

"Just a little lonely. Wishing you were here is all."

"Are you sure you don't want to come to Denver?" he asked.

This was why I didn't want to say anything. I sighed. "Yes, I am sure, there is no need for us to come to Denver."

"Okay. I'll be home before you know it. Why don't you get some sleep and I will talk to you in the morning?"

"Okay, good night. I love you."

"Love you too."

I hung up the phone and lay in bed staring at the TV and thinking of Spencer. I felt like I'd upset him by telling him what had happened. He wasn't acting like himself. Normally, by now, we'd have been hot and heavy into dirty talk, when instead he seemed to just want to get off the phone.

I arranged the covers partially over my naked body in such a way that would leave him wanting a little more and snapped a picture, which I sent straight to Spencer with the words 'wish you were here' attached to the message and hit send. It had barely been a minute when my phone vibrated, and I looked at the screen to see a crying emoji face. I couldn't help but laugh out loud.

RomanticAlpha42: Just wait till I get my hands on you.

BabyGirl89: Cannot wait ;)

Spencer

I glanced at my watch; it was already after seven and I was starving. I looked down at the menu, going over my options, while I waited for Max to arrive. It had been his suggestion to come here and, as usual, he was late.

It had been good to see my brother again. Over the years, we'd drifted apart, I'd married Brittany, and we'd had Nikki, while Max had gone off to find himself. Then I was in the middle of a horrible divorce. Mike and I would only hear from him occasionally, until he'd returned to the States.

This afternoon, I'd sat down with my brother to go over my plans for the Denver office, and over the course of two hours, I'd learned that Max had lied to me about everything. He'd lied about most of his experiences, and I also found out that he'd been fired from his last two jobs. I knew he was worried that I'd be firing him from this one, and I really should have, but when I realized how desperate he was to get this job, it changed my mind.

He'd only been back in the States for sixteen months when he'd woken one morning, no job, on the verge of getting evicted from his apartment, and heard a knock on his door. He'd opened it to find his ex-girlfriend, who'd walked out one morning, standing in front of him holding a baby. His baby. So yes, he'd been desperate.

I'd let out a breath. "Why is it you never told me all this to start?"

"I don't know. I needed something to get myself up in the morning. Everything fell apart when Pam left me. You know how that is, but when she showed up with the baby and dumped him on my lap, I was desperate. Are you going to fire me?"

I looked down at the reports I'd brought from the office back home and shook my head. "No, I will not fire you, Max. In all honesty, I did not know what I was doing when I started this company either. Most of it was trial and error, until I found most of my core team. I can train you, regardless of how angry I am. I still want you to be a part of this. I want to build a legacy."

Max chuckled. "A legacy, really. That is a really interesting way to put it."

No matter how angry I was, I still felt for him. However, we went over all the plans I had written for him, along with all the goals, and I planned to work with him to get him where he needed to be instead of taking the easy way out.

"Sorry I'm late," Max said, sliding into the booth across from me.

"That's okay. I hope you know what you want, because I am ready to chew my arm off." I chuckled.

Max reached for the menu and opened it, , closing it two minutes later while I signaled for the server.

"So, since you know all about my issues, tell me, how are things with you? How did the engagement thing go?" Max questioned.

"Went well. I still say it would have been nice for you to have been there, to meet Ainsley."

"Well, given the circumstances..."

"I know." The baby was the entire reason we hadn't heard from him. Instead of calling us, he'd kept all of that to himself, until today.

"I don't really get why you're rushing to get married to this chick. I mean, twenty years' difference in age is huge. What if she is just after your money?" Max questioned.

"She isn't after my money," I replied.

"Do you know that for a fact? Did you ask her to sign a prenup?"

I rolled my eyes. "No, Max, no prenup. We are in love."

"Yeah, in love, that is what I said about Pam, until she walked out on me and then walked back into my life with a baby. Just wait until she tells you she is pregnant." Max chuckled.

I grew quiet. "Well, Max, I don't need to wait for that." I sat back putting my hands behind my head.

"Are you fucking with me?"

"No, I'm not. Ainsley is pregnant."

"You got the sitter pregnant?" Max questioned, leaning forward, interested in whatever gossip he may find out.

"Careful, that is my soon-to-be wife you are speaking of," I gritted.

Max sat back. "True. Tell me, what could you possibly see in her long-term? Have you even thought about your future?"

"My future is all I think about, Max. Providing a home for Nikki and Ainsley and now the baby, maintaining the growth of the company."

"That may be, but have you thought about how you have absolutely nothing in common? I mean, in twenty years she'll be changing your diapers, for fuck sakes. She's gonna want to party, and you're going to want to go to bed at nine."

"Why don't you tell me how you really feel, Max?"

"Fuck, I am. It's the truth, Spencer."

I frowned. "I just told you to be careful. I've given you

a job, and only a few hours ago you were begging me to keep it. This is an opportunity for you to make a fresh start, to leave your past behind."

"I'm grateful, Spencer, really I am. I just..."

I put my hand up to stop him. The last thing Ainsley and I needed was yet another person who disapproved of our relationship. Max was my younger brother, and we'd only just reconnected a few months ago. He had no right to judge us. He was also my employee, and this type of talk needed to be stopped immediately.

"You will respect my decisions, Max. I'm in love with Ainsley. We are getting married, yes she is having my baby, and Nikki adores her. Honestly, had you of been around the last year or so or had shown up to our engagement party, you would probably feel the same way about her."

"I will do my best to keep my opinions to myself. And look... Nikki will have someone to grow up with."

I looked at my brother, unsure if that was a hit directed at Ainsley's age or if he was talking about the new baby.

"I really hope you are referring to the new baby," I gritted.

"Of course, that is what I meant. I am sure Ainsley is very mature for her age, 'cause lord knows she has to be because you don't have an immature bone in yours."

Ainsley

"All right, you, crawl in," I said, pulling the covers back so Nikki could climb into bed.

Nikki looked up at me, then grabbed two more stuffed animals from a pile in the corner. She carried them over to the bed and crawled in.

"You don't normally sleep with those," I said, taking notice that she left her favourite teddy bear on the floor by the door.

"Oh, can you get me Teddy?" Nikki cried, reaching her little arms out for the bear.

We'd gone through this every night since Spencer had been gone. I walked over and grabbed the bear and brought it to the edge of the bed, tucking her under the covers with all three of the stuffed animals. I kissed her on the forehead and was about to turn out the lights when Nikki sat up.

"Aren't you going to read me a story?"

I glanced at the clock to see it was almost eight thirty. Which meant it was already an hour past Nikki's bedtime. If she didn't get to sleep soon, she would be impossible to get up in the morning. "Not tonight, sweets. It's already past your bedtime. Now, you need to lie down and close your eyes and get some sleep," I said, pulling the covers up over her a little more.

"Just one," Nikki begged.

"No, sweetie, you need your rest. You have school in the morning."

"But I'm not tired."

"I beg to differ," I said, sitting down on the edge of her bed.

"Please, Ainsley."

"Nikki, what did your father say?" I questioned.

"Please, Ainsley, just one."

I bent down and kissed her forehead and then shook my head. "No, now go to sleep," I said, shutting her bedside light off. I walked over to her bedroom door and pulled it partway shut. "Good night."

"Night," she huffed.

I turned the small light on in the bathroom just outside Nikki's door and headed to the living room where Carly was searching through Netflix for a movie.

"I made popcorn. What do you feel like watching?" she questioned.

I took a handful and shoved the kernels in my mouth. "Something romantic," I said, flopping on the couch. "What about you?"

"True crime. I'm in the mood for blood and guts."

"Ugh, true crime? No wonder you're still single." I giggled.

"Romance!" Carly said, sticking her tongue out at me. "That is why you're pregnant. I'm comfortable and confident with my choices."

"As am I." We looked at one another and laughed.

Carly continued scrolling through choices. "Well, we will see how comfortable and confident you are in twenty years."

I rolled my eyes. I didn't want to hear it. I pulled the blanket off the back of the couch and threw it over my pajama-clad legs and took a sip of my coke.

"How about this?" Carly said, shoving the computer toward me to read the synopsis.

"Fine, that's fine. At least it isn't true crime. Drama will have to do."

"Since when are you against dramas?" Carly questioned as she started the movie.

I shrugged and rested my head on the back of the couch. "Since there is now enough drama in my life to satisfy an entire movie plot."

"Why?" she asked, pausing the movie. "What's gone on now?"

I had kept things quiet from Carly, since I knew how she felt about Spencer and me. I also didn't want to trouble her with my adult issues. However, I knew I needed to talk about things with someone other than Spencer. I let out a sigh and looked at my best friend.

"We will start by saying I really don't want to hear you say I told you so, but things haven't been so great. My father came home from his trip and found an invitation in his mailbox to the baby shower."

Carly's eyes widened. "Oh my God, Ainsley, I wondered where that one went."

"What do you mean?" I questioned.

"Well, remember you asked me to drop the mail off that you had gotten. I took it and shoved it all in the mailbox, and then...wait a minute." Carly got up and took off toward the front door. I heard it open, and after a few minutes she returned, her face as white as a ghost.

"What is it?"

"It was my fault. I took the mail over, and when I got back in my car, I just took the top envelope off the pile of invites and shoved it in my glove box. Which was where I'd put your father's, so I didn't mail it. I never even looked at the name. I just took the pile to the post office and mailed them. I just looked now, and it was Jenna's invite in my glove box, not your dad's. I bet I grabbed it when I put the mail in the mailbox," Carly said, covering her mouth. "I'm so sorry, Ainsley. Please forgive me."

Carly stood there in near tears, staring at me. I knew no matter how much she disapproved of our relationship, she would never do something like this on purpose. "I forgive you."

She took a moment and wiped her eyes. "So, what happened?" Carly asked, sitting back down beside me.

"He came over here and got angry. Then he saw the banner that Spencer and Nikki had made for the night we got the house. He blew up. Demanded I come home."

Carly looked at me, almost shocked that my father had found out about the baby and the house in such a short period. "You mean he found everything out that night?"

"Yep, in about ten minutes. Ten minutes, he learned we were having a baby and that we were moving. He demanded that I return home, which I didn't, and now he won't speak to me."

"It's your dad. I am sure he will come around."

I shrugged. "I hope so. However, that isn't all of it. Brittany hasn't exactly been wonderful either. She was the server at the restaurant we had gone to the night you stayed and watched Nikki. She attacked me and Spencer and ended up losing her job. I ran into her yesterday at the coffee shop inside the bookstore, and she attacked me again there as well."

"What the hell is with that woman?"

"I don't know."

"Do you think she wants him back?" Carly questioned.

"I don't think so. I mean, she cheated on Spencer, so I am just thinking she either really hates the pair of us or she hates herself for what she let go."

"Maybe, perhaps, she wants him back. You know, she realizes what it is she lost."

I shrugged. "Perhaps."

"The fact that she cheated on him doesn't really mean anything. Perhaps they were going through a dry spell. I mean, he is old."

"Ugh, please. Don't start with the age thing again, please,"

"I'm only saying I read an article in *Cosmo* about men in their forties, and that sometimes they have a hard time, you know, getting it up," Carly said.

I rolled my eyes. "Don't worry, Carly, there isn't any dry spell. He has no problems. In fact, he loves to—"

Carly held her hands over her ears and closed her eyes. "I don't want to know. Now what else?"

"The venues still haven't called us back. I spent all morning calling them and no one would take my calls. Plus, we close on the house in about three weeks. Possibly two now, and this place isn't even on the market yet."

"Whoa, relax. I'm sure Spencer has everything under control."

"I know. I am trying to calm myself down. It's just I look around and every which way I turn, it's one disaster after another," I said, a tear slipping down my cheek.

"Okay. We are coming up with a plan of attack. Tomorrow, after we take Nikki to school, you and I are going to go to the places you've called. We are going to find you a location for your wedding," Carly said, taking hold of my hands in hers. "I want to see my best friend smile again."

"Thank you." I sniffled. "It means the world to me."

"Of course. I'll also lay off on the Spencer attacks. He really isn't that bad of a guy. Now let's relax and watch this movie."

Spencer

The cab pulled into our driveway, and I paid the driver as he pulled my bags out of the trunk. I'd never been so happy to return home. The trip to Denver was great. Not only had it given me a chance to help Max with the Denver division, but it had given us the chance to spend some time together.

I waited for the cab to pull out of the driveway before turning and looking up at the house. Most lights were off, except for the ones in the front windows. I was excited to see Ainsley and had hoped she was still awake. I'd done the best I could to get home at a decent hour, but with the weather delay, that hadn't been possible.

I walked up to the door and slid my key in the lock, opening the front door. Soft music filled the house. I smiled. Ainsley normally had music playing when she was working in the evening. I knew she hadn't been in the office much while I'd been gone, so I figured she was probably playing catchup. I put my bags down and climbed the stairs and poked my head into the kitchen to find her standing at the counter plating food.

"Hey, sexy," I whispered as I stepped up behind her and wrapped my arms around her.

She rested her head on my shoulder, a smile coming to her lips. "Well, this isn't how you were supposed to find out about dinner. I must have timed your drive back wrong," she said, placing the pot back on the stove before turning in my arms. "I missed you," she said in a low voice as her arms rested on my shoulders and she met my lips, her body fitting perfectly against mine.

"I missed you too," I whispered, pulling her tighter against me before kissing her again. "What's all this?" I questioned, reaching over her shoulder and grabbing a carrot off one plate.

"This is dinner. I hope you're hungry."

"I'm starving, actually. They didn't offer food on the flight back because of the weather. The turbulence was brutal. Can I help you with anything?"

"Nope. I have it all taken care of. Why don't you take a minute, get comfortable and then go have a seat in the dining room and I will bring in dinner."

"I can do that." I placed a kiss on the side of her neck and listened as she giggled.

"Did you want me to make you a drink?" she questioned.

I shook my head. "No, I got it. I'll just pour myself a scotch," I said, pressing my lips to hers one more time.

I grabbed a rock glass from the cabinet and placed three cubes of ice into it and headed into the dining room, where I poured myself a glass and took a seat in my usual spot.

"Here we are," she said, setting a plate in front of me." I looked down at the carrots, asparagus, and chicken.

"This looks amazing."

"Thanks. I wanted to make you something special for tonight," she said, sitting down in her usual spot beside me.

I smiled. "Thank you. Everything go okay while I was gone?" I questioned. I'd been worried about leaving her to begin with, and once I knew she had run into Brittany, it had made it worse. It still bothered me that I hadn't just taken them both with me instead. I also knew that Ainsley could lie to me over the phone, however face-to-face, I could read her like a book. I knew when she was sad, upset, worried, and frustrated, her eyes gave everything away.

"Yeah, everything went fine. Of course, Nikki tried to push boundaries, but then she always did when you'd leave me with her. This time though I feel it's different."

"Yeah, I am going to have to talk to her about that."

"Ah, maybe she is just being a kid. It's fine. She was a little tired today. She didn't want to go to bed last night, and she was up later than she should have been tonight. So, when I put her down tonight, again, there was no bedtime story."

"That's okay. She will live without a story for a couple of nights. I know what she can be like when she gets cranky. I swear Brittany just lets her do whatever she wants when she is with her. I've also been noticing that every time she comes back from there, she never wants to sleep. She also gets demanding."

"Yeah, I have a feeling it's because she's ignoring her. You should have seen how she acted, Nikki was trying to tell her something and she wouldn't even look at her."

"Well, I'll address that when I have a chat with Brittany. I also need to mention it to my lawyer."

"How did things go with Max?"

"Okay, nothing that we couldn't correct. He also sends his apologies for not making it to our engagement party."

Ainsley shrugged. "It doesn't matter, but you can tell him thank you."

I watched her drag her fork around her plate, moving pieces of carrots and asparagus around, not really eating. "Did you hear anything from the venues?"

Ainsley let out a deep sigh. "No, nothing. Nor from

the caterers. Carly and I went to all of them today as well. I think I am just going to look up some different places."

"Sure, never hurts to do that. We could always try contacting the one we used for the Christmas party. It's always an option."

"I'll do that. Oh, you should have seen Nikki at the mall. We went into the bedding store, and she found the bedding she wanted immediately. That was until she spotted three others that she liked as well. I spent twenty-five minutes letting her try to decide on the one she wanted, only to end up deciding for her by bribing her with a set of purple sheets," Ainsley said, hiding her face in her hands and laughing.

I let out a laugh. I knew how Nikki could be. "Well, I am glad you two figured it out and had a great time. I'm also glad that you decided for her, otherwise you might still be there." I chuckled, setting my fork and knife down on my plate.

"We did. She's been asking to use everything since we got it. So, I compromised. I feared if I didn't, she'd never go to bed. I allowed her to use the heart-shaped pillow I got for her."

"Heart-shaped pillow?"

"Yep, she wanted it to go with her blanket." Ainsley laughed.

I was glad to see Ainsley appeared to be in better

spirits than when I'd spoken to her the other night. I looked into her eyes; she looked tired, which I expected.

She reached for my plate, but I put my hand on hers, stopping her. "Why don't I clean everything up and you head down to the bedroom and get ready for bed?"

She looked at the dirty dishes in front of us. "The kitchen is clean. Everything is in the dishwasher. It will only take me a couple of seconds. Besides, you've travelled all day."

"And you've been looking after everything here."

She looked around. "Will you be in soon?"

"I'm going to pop these in the dishwasher and then I'll be right behind you," I said, taking her hand in mine and bringing it to my lips.

She looked at everything before reluctantly getting up and starting down the hall toward the bedroom. I took a few moments and wiped the counters down and put the rest of the food away, then I shut out the lights and headed down the hall to the bedroom.

When I walked in, the two bedside table lights were on, and the door to the bathroom was ajar. I placed my bag down on my nightstand and quickly got out of my clothes. I'd just hung up my suit and was just about to unpack my bag when Ainsley appeared in the bathroom's doorway.

I glanced her way and did a double take. Ainsley stood before me wearing a very sexy black lace lingerie set I'd never seen before. My mouth watered at the sight of her, and my cock instantly hardened.

Her eyes locked with mine as she slowly made her way over to me. I'd never seen her eyes so full of want, need, and sex all at the same time. She trailed her fingers down my chest, stopping at the top of my boxers. "I missed you," she whispered, running her hand over my bulge.

"I missed you too," I said, my voice cracking at her touch.

She pressed her lips to mine and her body into me. I grabbed her. Picking her up, I carried her over to the bed and placed her down on the edge. She lay back on the mattress as my eyes roamed her body. "When did you get this?" I asked, my fingers tracing over the lacy material.

"Do you like it?" she asked, innocently looking up at me.

I gripped her thighs and pulled her to the edge of the bed. Standing between her legs, I pushed myself against her. "Does it feel like I don't like it?" I growled.

Instantly, the innocence washed from her eyes and in place of that I saw nothing but heat, want, and desire. I met her lips and kissed her hard, making my way to that soft spot on her neck. I felt her body weaken as I concentrated on that little spot she loved. When I heard that little moan, I pushed her body back onto the bed.

I looked down at her. Her eyes were begging me for more. I kneeled on the bed and held my body weight with one hand as I bent down and licked her nipple through the lace, then gently bit and sucked it into my mouth.

Arching her back, pushing herself farther into my mouth, Ainsley let out a moan that sent a wave through my body. I gripped my hardened cock, hoping that I could relieve some pressure. I repeated the process with the other and then ran my finger between her legs.

She looked up at me as my fingers danced over the now soaked piece of fabric that covered her.

"Don't tease," she whimpered.

"Teasing is half the fun," I whispered, using just enough pressure so she could feel me there.

I met her lips, my tongue washing through her mouth as her fingers gripped my back. "Slide up into bed," I whispered.

She did as I asked, moving into the centre of the bed. I kissed my way down her body and moved between her legs, pushing them open. I ran my fingers once again over that square piece of fabric, again pushing just hard enough I knew she could feel me.

"Don't tease me," she cried, gripping the blanket under her.

I smiled. I loved it when she begged me. I slid that little piece of fabric to the side and ran my finger through her wet center. She sucked in a breath and arched her back as my finger ran over the bundle of nerves again and again, before sliding two fingers deep inside of her.

"Am I teasing you now?" I whispered as I leaned down to her ear, gently biting her earlobe while fucking her with my fingers.

Her only response was another moan as my thumb circled the small bundle of nerves as my fingers curled inside her. Her hand gripped my arm, and she met my lips, kissing me hard as she moaned louder this time.

I could feel her tightening, so I pulled my fingers from inside her and pulled my aching cock from my boxers. She looked up at me and watched as I stroked myself, my eyes meeting hers.

I slid the little pair of panties down her body and threw them to the floor, then spread her legs open a little farther, lining myself up at her entrance. "You want this?" I asked, pushing just hard enough to enter her a tiny bit.

She bit her bottom lip and nodded her head.

I pushed inside, burying myself in her. Instantly, I met her lips as I thrust into her. Wrapping my arms around her, I held her tightly against me, kissing her as I slowed my pace. I rolled onto my back, pulling her on top of me.

She pulled the rest of the lacy garment over her head and placed it beside her, then she rested her hands on my chest. My eyes ran down her body. I placed my hands on her hips, slowing her and guiding her movement.

I watched as nothing but pure pleasure lined her face. I loved watching her. "Does it feel good, baby?" I asked, breathing heavily.

The inhale of breath between her closed lips told me all I needed to know as she continued at the pace I'd set for her. She closed her eyes, her head dropping back as she rolled her hips. "God, yes," she cried.

I sat up and wrapped my arms around her and guided her, slowing her down as I felt her tighten around me. She buried her face in my neck, her hot breath tickling me as she started moving a little faster.

She interlaced her fingers with mine as her breathing quickened, and her head dropped back as she screamed my name. As soon as she called my name, I couldn't hold back any longer, and I poured into her, holding her close.

Ainsley

The afternoon sun poured through the windows behind me. The office was buzzing today; the phone hadn't stopped ringing since we'd gotten in, and Spencer hadn't had a second to himself all morning. I got up from my chair and pulled the blinds down behind me so I could see my computer screen a little easier. I glanced at the clock; it was a little after two and I still hadn't heard from my father.

I'd placed a call to him earlier this morning, as Spencer had suggested. He wanted us to have dinner together, to clear the air, so I'd called and invited my father and Jane over tomorrow evening. Jane had tried to get my father on the phone, but he refused to take the call and instead she said she would talk to him.

I was about to get up and head down to the washroom when my phone rang. I grabbed it, hoping that it would be my father, but disappointment flooded me. It was the last venue I'd contacted. They finally returned my call to tell me they, too, had no availability for us. The other ones had left voice messages over the weekend. This one was our last option. I swallowed hard. I could feel the tears building as I put the phone down.

"Don't cry here," I muttered to myself. "It's unprofessional." I rubbed my temples, like I did when I had a headache.

I wiped at my eyes just as Spencer's office door opened and two men stepped out into the hall, with Spencer following. He didn't look over my way, thank goodness, so I covered my eyes and pretended to be working on something when the phone rang again. This time it was the caterer, and once again, they broke the news that they were fully booked right into the later part of the summer.

Completely defeated, I stood up and stretched just as Spencer rounded the corner. "What time is your doctor's appointment at?" he questioned.

I glanced at the clock. "In twenty-five minutes."

"Why didn't you send me a reminder?"

"I reminded you this morning over breakfast. You said you put it in your calendar."

"Give me five minutes," Spencer grumbled under his breath before going into his office and shutting the door.

I frowned. It wasn't like him to be so grumpy, especially toward me. Ten minutes later, we were in his car, heading toward the medical building five blocks away.

We now sat in the small exam room. My stomach felt uneasy as we waited for the doctor to come in. I pulled my phone from my jacket pocket and looked to see if I had missed any calls, hoping that my father had attempted to call me back, but still nothing.

"Hasn't called yet, has he?" Spencer questioned.

I shook my head and shoved the phone back into my pocket, then I slipped out of my coat, passing it to Spencer. "No. I don't think he will," I said, looking toward the floor and swallowing hard, hoping I didn't break out in tears.

"Hello." The door opened and in walked Dr. Pines. "Ainsley, how are we feeling today?" she questioned as she sat down behind the small desk and turned on the computer screen.

"Good, thanks," I lied.

Spencer glanced at me. I could tell from the look on his face he knew I wasn't telling her the truth, and I hoped he said nothing.

"Spencer, how are things?" Dr. Pines asked.

"Good, thanks."

"Good, so shall we get started?" She came around with a blood pressure cuff. "Just want to get a blood pressure reading first."

"The nurse already did that," I replied, looking at Spencer.

"Well, the first reading was a little high, so I want to take it again now that you've been sitting here for a while. Hold out your arm."

She wrapped the cuff around my arm. "Relax," she said as the cuff tightened. She watched, frowning. "It's higher than I'd like to see at this stage," she said, going back around to her chair and typing into the computer. "Have you been experiencing any stress?"

Spencer looked at me and waited for me to say something, only I kept quiet.

"Ainsley?" Dr. Pines questioned. "Have you been experiencing any stress?"

I knew Spencer would probably say something if I didn't, so I slowly nodded my head. "Yes. I'm also a little nervous."

"Nothing to be nervous about. I also noticed that your weight is a little low as well. Have you been eating okay?"

"Yes."

"Actually," Spencer jumped in, "she barely eats on a good day."

Dr. Pines looked over at me. "Ainsley, you need to eat. Especially now. I see from your family doctor that you've always had an issue eating, especially when you're experiencing stress."

I nodded. "Yes, that is true." In the time Spencer and I were apart after my father found us, I'd lost almost twenty pounds in a month. I still hadn't put all that weight back on and then I found out I was pregnant.

"Okay, so we will go over a healthy diet before you go today. Now, how about you lay back?" Dr. Pines said with a smile as she pulled a tray with a machine on it behind her. "I want to take a peek at this baby. If we are lucky, we may even hear a heartbeat. I'll just have you slip in behind that screen in the corner and put the gown on, open at the front."

I did as she requested and when I came back out, the doctor had already adjusted the table so I could lie down a little more. I walked over and climbed back up, Spencer coming over to my side and taking hold of my hand as I lay back.

She placed a blanket over my legs. "Now, we will just open your gown a little. You can leave your breasts covered."

I did as she asked. She squirted some cold jelly onto my belly. Then she took a wand and rubbed it over my abdomen.

She studied the monitor, moving the wand slowly over my abdomen. "There we go," she said, pointing to the screen.

"Is that it?" I asked, trying to see something that resembled a baby.

"That is it." Dr. Pines smiled, pointing to the monitor as she continued to move the wand over my abdomen, pressing a little harder than before. "Let's see if we can get a heartbeat."

A frown came to her face as she moved the wand, and I got a little worried. "Is there something wrong?" I questioned, lifting my back off the table.

"No, Ainsley, just relax."

Spencer tightened his hold on my hand and brought a kiss to my forehead, trying to comfort me, but I was growing increasingly worried that something wasn't right from the look on the doctor's face.

"Why haven't we heard the heartbeat?" I asked, alarm in my voice.

"Well, sometimes we can't hear it just yet. It's nothing to be concerned about," she said, turning the monitor closer to her as she continued waving the wand over my stomach at a slower pace. "We will set up another appointment for two weeks from now. Lots of times I can't get a heartbeat this early. Doesn't necessarily mean something is wrong."

She shut the machine off and passed me a cloth, and I quickly wiped up the jelly. Spencer held my hand while I got off the table and went and got changed. When I returned, I sat beside Spencer.

"Now, I'd like to talk to you about restrictions. First, I am printing out a healthy selection of foods that I want you to make sure you are eating. Also, a portion guide. I also want as little stress as possible for you. Do you know what some stresses are?" Dr. Pines asked, quickly making a note. "Is it family?"

I gave a small nod. "How did you guess?"

Dr. Pines smiled. "Well, you aren't the first couple I've had that have had such a difference in age. Plus, your family doctor filled me in on a few things."

I nodded again. "I see."

"So, I'd like you to limit those visits with the ones who are the primary cause of those stressors."

I nodded and looked at Spencer, who softly smiled and winked.

"Is there any reason that stress could harm the baby?" I questioned.

"Well, stress isn't good for any of us. I tell all my patients to limit their stress triggers." She smiled. "Also, I don't want you lifting anything heavier than twenty-five pounds."

My head shot up and my eyes met hers.

"Is that an issue?" she questioned.

"We are moving. I have to lift. I have boxes to pack and unpack."

Spencer cleared his throat. "We have a moving company coming to pack and move us. If need be, I'll have them unpack as well. Ainsley, you can supervise," Spencer replied.

"Problem solved," Dr. Pines said, smiling at me.

On the inside, I felt like screaming, but I sat there, listening to the things Dr. Pines said. I prayed this appointment was soon going to be over. I somewhat felt like I was being attacked, and I could feel the stress and worry piling on until I began feeling unwell. I swallowed hard as she finally stood up from behind her desk and handed Spencer a few pages that she'd printed.

"I want to see you in two weeks. We will have another ultrasound during that appointment. You can book at the front desk before you leave."

I nodded and took Spencer's hand. As soon as the doctor was gone, Spencer and I made our way out to reception. I was just as happy to call and book, but Spencer stopped at the small desk and waited.

Once the appointment was booked we headed out of the office. We were just about to the car when I felt my phone vibrate in my pocket. I removed it to see a text from Jane waiting for me. I stopped walking and my hand shook as I typed in my password.

"What is it?" Spencer questioned.

"Jane messaged me," I said, swallowing hard as I read the message. "Jane says Dad won't come for dinner." I swallowed hard, my eyes burning.

"Perfect. Just perfect," Spencer muttered under his breath.

"How is that perfect?" I cried.

Spencer looked at me. "Ainsley, I didn't mean it that way."

I looked down at my phone as the words Jane had written blurred in front of me. A tear slipped down my cheek and my throat got tight. "Limit the stress. Easier said than done," I whispered to myself.

Spencer wrapped his arms around me. "I don't want you worrying about anything," he whispered. "If your dad is going to be that way, let him. If he doesn't want to come to the wedding, that is fine. However, if he does, and he creates a scene, I will ask them both to leave."

Alarm filled me. "You will?"

"Yes, it is our wedding, and you are going to be my wife. I will not let him treat you like a child at our wedding or in our own home. Now, chin up. We are going to get your weight up, and the house will get packed, and things between you and your father will get straightened out. It's up to him now to decide which path he would rather take," he said, kissing my lips.

Ainsley

Rain hit the large window, while I sat on the couch replying to an email. A large rumble of thunder followed by a flash of lightning tore my attention away from my laptop. It had been cloudy and rainy for the past three days, totally matching my mood.

I was just about to get up and check on the people who were packing things up in the house when my phone dinged with a message. I looked down and smiled.

ROMANTICALPHA42: How are things?

BABYGIRL89: Going well. They are just about done with Nikki's room.

I'd been working from home for the past two days while the packing company Spencer hired came into the house and began packing things. They would pack up a room or two and then they would load things into their van and take them over to the new house and unpack.

BABYGIRL89: How are things going at the office?

ROMANTICALPHA42: Busy. As always.

BABYGIRL89: Great. I think Brittany called here today.

ROMANTICALPHA42: She's been calling the office all morning.

BABYGIRL89: Phone is ringing again.

ROMANTICALPHA42: Just ignore her. I'll be home in an hour.

I put my phone down and laptop on the table just as one girl who was packing came into the living room.

"We are just about finished with the basement and the little girl's room. Tomorrow we will tackle this room, the spare room, and the garage. Then on Saturday we will finish the last four rooms to have you completely moved in for moving day."

"That sounds perfect. Did you need me to come over to the new house with you when you take this load?"

"No, miss. Mr. Brooks went over where everything goes."

I nodded. "Thank you for everything."

"You are welcome."

I watched as she made her way back down the hall and turned into the small bathroom outside of Nikki's room and got busy while two of the others began taking boxes out to their van.

> BABYGIRL89: You'll be happy to know that everything will be done by moving day. They are finishing everything up over the weekend.

While I stood there waiting for a reply, I heard a knock at the front door. I put my phone down and walked down the three steps, pulling the door open. My father stood there in the rain, soaking wet, with a sad look on his face. I was so shocked to see him standing there, all I could do was stare.

"You have a couple minutes for your old man?" he questioned; his hands shoved in his pockets.

I didn't know what to say. All I wanted was for him to wrap his arms around me and tell me everything was okay between us. When I didn't respond, he hung his head.

"I don't blame you. I'll be on my way."

I watched him turn and walk across the driveway. "Daddy, wait," I called.

He turned back around and came running over to the door. I stepped to the side, allowing him enough room to come inside. I shut the door behind him and immediately he wrapped his arms around me and pulled me in for the biggest hug he'd ever given me.

"Daddy, I am so sorry," I cried, hugging him just as tight for a moment before I slowly released my grip and took a step back.

"Ainsley, I'd like you to come back home." He muttered, "Please."

Shocked, I stood there staring back at my father. "Daddy, I'm not coming back home."

"Ainsley, please."

"No, Daddy. We are getting married, we are having a baby. Your grandbaby," I said, crossing my arms in front of my chest. I felt I had to remain strong and stand my ground. I was by myself in this for the moment, at least until Spencer arrived.

"Ainsley, I just want to talk."

"I don't need to come home for that. We can talk here."

He was silent for a moment, and he shifted his weight from one foot to the other. "I want to know why it is you both felt you couldn't tell me the truth?"

"Do you really have to ask that?" I questioned. "Dad, you haven't been the most understanding person about any of this."

"Understanding? You want me to be understanding?"

"Yes," I practically shouted, then remembered that I had the packers in the house.

"Ainsley, do you have any idea how shocking this has been? I mean, I come home in the middle of the night. Go to check on you and find my daughter in bed with a man that I trusted to look after you while I was gone."

"You're acting as if he was babysitting me. I'm twenty years old, Dad. I babysit his daughter."

"Fine, 'look after' is the wrong way to put it. However, I find you, wrapped in his arms, naked. A man my age. What was I supposed to say, that everything is all right, just keep fucking my daughter?"

My mouth flew open at his choice of words. My father had never spoken to me like that. "Dad, please."

"No, Ainsley, you are a grownup. Tell me what the hell was I supposed to think? Why else would a man my age have any interest in a girl your age? You were nothing more than something he could fuck."

My eyes filled with tears at his choice of words. Then anger filled me. "Did you ever think that the way you react to things was the reason we didn't tell you?"

"The way I react!"

"Yes, you found out about the baby through an invitation not even addressed to you. Then you barged over here and demanded I move back home without even asking us if it was true. You just assumed. I'm not coming back home." I crossed my arms over my chest and stood there staring at my father, reeling with hurt and anger.

My father looked at me, worry crossing his face. "I really hope you aren't making a huge mistake, Ainsley. I hope I am wrong."

Just then, the front door opened, and Spencer stepped inside to find me glaring at my father. Without so much as a word to Spencer, my father shoved past him and left the house. Spencer took one look at me. "What the hell was that about?"

I shook my head. "I don't know. I thought he was coming here to apologize."

"What happened?"

"I told him I wasn't coming home, and then he reminded me of all the reasons I didn't want to tell him the truth about the baby right away." My eyes filled with tears as I stood there looking at the closed door. "Do you ever think he will come around?"

"I don't know. I'd like to say yes," Spencer said, wrapping his arm around me and pulling me into his chest.

Spencer

Once I'd gotten Ainsley calmed down, we went into the kitchen and prepared a meal together. I'd wanted to do whatever it took to get her mind off what had happened, and so far it had worked.

We ate in the kitchen as the dining room table was now covered in boxes and glassware. We'd just finished our meal, and I sat back in my chair and took a drink. "So, you said that everything will be done in time?"

"That is what they told me."

"Well, that went better than I expected. We should take a drive over to the new place tonight and check on things."

"Sure." Ainsley shrugged.

"All right then, give me a few minutes and we will head out."

I cleared the table and shoved the dishes into the dishwasher. Then we made our way out to the car. I pulled my seatbelt across me, while Ainsley did the same, and then I noticed she shifted uncomfortably in her seat at the same time she let out a small moan.

"What is it?" I questioned.

"Nothing, I just got a sharp pain in my back is all. I must have pinched something," she said, moving around while trying to get comfortable.

"You sure that is all?"

"Yes. See, it's all better now," she said, finally sitting still.

I drove off toward the new house, pulling into the driveway in ten minutes. I came around to Ainsley's side of the car and opened the door, helping her out, and together we walked to the front door while looking at the gardens. I slid the key into the lock and we stepped inside. Some rooms contained boxes and others had the furniture all set up. We headed upstairs to the bedrooms and found Nikki's almost completed.

"Wow, it looks amazing," Ainsley said.

"Yes, this company was highly recommended. They have done an amazing job so far, haven't they?"

I watched as Ainsley walked across the room and flipped the light on the inside of Nikki's own bathroom. "Wow, I really think Nikki is going to love this. What about you?" She was about to take a step when, once again, she flinched in pain, this time putting her hand on her abdomen.

"Ainsley, what is it?" I asked, rushing over to her.

"Just that same pain again."

I frowned, worried that something was wrong. "I think we should get back to the house. I think a hot bath and bed are for you."

It surprised me she didn't fight me but agreed. That worried me more. Concern lined my face; she took my hand and together we made our way back out of the house and drove back home.

Once home, I drew her a hot bath and got her settled, and then I headed into the living room to do some work. I'd just gotten off the phone with Max when I heard a bang come from the bedroom. I listened hard, but heard nothing, so I went back to what I'd been working on. I was just about to call Max back when I was sure I heard my name.

I got up and began walking down to the bedroom; halfway down the hall I heard Ainsley scream. I took off, shoving the bedroom door open, and ran into our ensuite to find Ainsley sitting on the bathroom floor, naked. Her legs and hand covered in blood.

"Spencer," she cried, looking down at her hand, then her legs. "I...I...I...don't know what is wrong."

Immediately, I dropped to my knees and grabbed the towel off the edge of the tub, wiping her hand. I reached and grabbed the towel that hung on the towel rack and covered her legs and pulled my cell phone from my pocket immediately dialing the emergency line.

Her body shook as she leaned against me, listening as I made the emergency call. I held her close, waiting for what seemed to take forever for the ambulance to arrive.

I'd been waiting in this damn waiting room for over two hours and had heard nothing. I paced back and forth frantically. I was just about to sit down when a nurse walked by the room.

"Excuse me," I called, and then repeated, "Excuse me."

"Sir?" She came back into view.

"I'm here with Ainsley Matthews. Has there been any updates?" I questioned.

"I'm sorry, sir, I don't know. I'm not looking after anyone by that name. I can check with the nurses' station and find out for you if you like."

I could feel my heart beating in my ears and nodded. "Thank you."

The nurse turned around and went back the way she came. I took a seat on the couch and picked up a magazine off the table, flipping through it, barely seeing anything. They'd taken her from the paramedics the second I'd walked through the emergency room doors. I didn't even have time to say anything to her, to let her know I was here, nothing. They just whisked her off as she lay on the stretcher, clutching her body, crying in pain.

I'd sent a message to Carly a little over an hour ago and still had heard nothing from her. I dropped the magazine on the table just as the nurse returned to the doorway.

"I'm sorry, sir. There have been no updates yet," the nurse said quietly and continued to walk down the hall.

I felt helpless, completely powerless at this moment. I always had control. I wasn't used to this. I leaned back in the chair and stared at the wall when I heard my name quietly called from behind me. I turned and looked over my shoulder to see Carly, Jon, and Jane standing together. Sadness lined all their faces, along with worry.

"How is she?" Carly questioned.

My eyes travelled from her to Jane and then to Jon, who looked more worried than any of them combined.

"I... I don't know. I haven't heard a thing," I said, the first tear escaping from my eyes. I covered my mouth and turned my back. I just needed a minute to calm myself and take everything in that had happened in the past few hours. I never cried, but when I felt a small hand on my shoulder and turned around to see Carly standing there, her eyes full of tears, my own tears fell.

She wrapped her arms around me, and we stood there, the pair of us crying. "I just love her so fucking much," I whispered, feeling as if my heart were being ripped from my chest. "I don't know what I'll do if she isn't okay."

"She is going to be fine. Don't talk like that. She is going to be fine," Carly cried.

I pulled away from her and saw Jon and Jane standing in the same spot they had been. Jon had his arm around Jane, and they both had tears in their eyes. Carly guided me over to a chair, and the four of us sat down together.

We talked for a while, going over what happened, each of them listening, and then I heard my name called. I turned to see Doctor Pines standing in the doorway. "Spencer, can I see you please?"

Carly softly smiled and nodded at me. "Go... we'll be here."

I looked at Jon; he nodded as I got up from my chair, feeling the weight of everything on my shoulders.

"We'll be here, Spencer," Carly called out again, reassuring me they weren't going anywhere.

I turned and looked at her over my shoulder. "Thank you."

I walked over to where Doctor Pines stood. "Walk with me," she said.

We began walking down the hall toward a bank of rooms and stopped at the first one where I could see

Ainsley lying in the bed sleeping. "She's been asking for you."

I swallowed hard; I wanted to know what had happened, but I was afraid to ask. I was afraid to hear the answer, because somehow, I already knew the truth. Instead, I just stood there watching her.

"Do you want to know?" she asked. "Or would you prefer I let Ainsley tell you?"

"Is the baby... okay?" I questioned, the words getting stuck in my throat. I needed to be prepared in case the outcome wasn't good. I needed to be prepared to be strong for Ainsley.

Doctor Pines looked at me, a sullen look on her face. "I'm afraid not, Spencer. She lost the baby," she whispered.

My chest hurt as what Doctor Pines said registered in my mind. I looked through the doorway at the love of my life lying in the bed all alone. My thoughts drifted back to when she told me about the baby, how scared she was at how I'd react and how surprised she was when I didn't blow up. Then the complete look of excitement and happiness on her face.

"What happened? Do you think stress caused this?" I questioned.

"Most likely a chromosomal abnormality. I've seen this many times, and I have sent some tissue for testing to see if that is indeed the reason. Elevated cortisol can speed up the inevitable, but stress is not the cause, Spencer. While stress isn't good for her, or anyone for that fact, this is quite common to happen. About eighty percent of pregnancies end in miscarriage this early on."

I grew quiet as I watched Ainsley. "Will we ever be able to have children?" I asked.

"Yes, of course. She is perfectly healthy. I am going to set up an appointment for you guys to come in and speak with me at my office once the test results are back. I am not sure how Ainsley is going to take this. She knows, of course, but it's too early to tell how it may affect her psychologically. However, there is also a slight chance she won't be affected at all. Either way we can set her up with some therapy."

I nodded, still watching her through the window. I wanted to hold her, to make everything okay for her, but I knew that was impossible. This wasn't something I could put into a spreadsheet, tweak and fix.

"Go be with her. She has been asking for you since she woke," Doctor Pines said, placing her hand on my back. "I am truly sorry for your loss."

"Thank you," I whispered.

I stepped into her room, listening to the gentle beeping of her heart rate monitor. I made my way around the bed and gently took her hand in mine. I bent down and brushed her hair from her forehead and kissed her. She didn't move. I had just sat down in the chair beside her bed when a nurse came in and swapped out the almost empty IV bag, adjusted a couple of things on one machine and printed a report from another. She said nothing. She just gave me a nod and quietly left the room.

I brought Ainsley's hand to my lips and kissed the back of it, and she let out a small moan and slowly opened her eyes, blinking fast. She looked over at me. "Where are we?" she questioned, looking around the room.

"At the hospital, baby girl," I replied. "In your room."

It was then that her eyes filled with tears, and the once gentle beeping of the heart rate monitor got faster and a little louder. "Spencer, I'm so sorry, I lost the baby."

I wiped the tears that slid down her cheek and placed a kiss on her forehead. "I know," I said, swallowing hard. "It's not your fault," I whispered.

She tried to move closer to me but she couldn't, so I lowered the rail on the side of her bed. She was over far enough that I could lie beside her, so I carefully climbed onto the bed, sliding my arm under her and wrapping myself around her.

I'd just gotten comfortable when the door opened, and a nurse stepped inside. "Everything okay in here?" she asked, silencing the alarm on Ainsley's heart monitor.

I nodded, holding Ainsley tight against me. That was when I noticed that people from the hallway could see into the room. I didn't want them staring, watching us, as we shared this private moment together. "Nurse, could you please pull the curtain closed give us a little privacy?"

"Certainly, sir," she said, pulling the curtain over the glass window. "If you need anything, just hit the call button, okay," she said before leaving the room.

As soon as the nurse was gone, Ainsley shifted onto her side and wrapped her arm around me, burying herself in my chest. A guttural sob escaped her. Once again there was nothing I could do but hold her tight, allowing her to cry, to grieve for what we'd just lost.

A few hours had gone by. Ainsley was now sound asleep on her back. I slipped from the hospital bed and headed down the hall. I'd forgotten that Carly, Jon, and Jane were still there. I rounded the corner in time to see the three of them look up.

"How is she?" Carly asked immediately. "How is the baby?"

I looked at them, feeling empty. "She is okay. She, um..." I pinched the bridge of my nose and closed my eyes, "She lost the baby," I muttered. It was the first time I'd said those words. I'd heard them, I'd thought about them, a lot, but this was the first time I'd actually said them.

Carly covered her mouth as tears ran down her cheeks. Jane grabbed her and wrapped her arms around her, and she grabbed Jon's hand.

I stood there, watching as each one of them consoled the other, wishing that there was someone to console me. I turned around, sitting down on a chair away from them all. I buried my face in my hands as I listened to Carly cry. Jane was doing her best to calm her down.

I ran my fingers through my hair and let out a breath, and that was when I felt a firm hand on my shoulder. I sat there for a moment before looking up to see Jon staring down at me.

"I was wrong."

When I said nothing, he came around and sat down.

"I was wrong about you. About how you feel about her. I see it now."

It was wrong that it had taken this to get him to see my feelings for her. To lose a life in order for him to realize that I really, truly loved his daughter. I didn't have words. I wanted to shout at him but knew it would do no good. We'd all lost something here. It wasn't just Ainsley's and my loss; it was also Carly's, Jane's and Jon's.

It would take all of us time to heal. Heal from this, heal from the words that had been spoken. It would take us time to rebuild our relationships with one another. Everything now hinged on time.

Ainsley

4 months later

Spencer and I had spent the last four months working through what we'd lost. It had taken me a while to realize that it was nothing I had done. Doctor Pines had gotten the results back from the tissue samples she'd sent to the lab, and they confirmed it was a genetic abnormality that caused the miscarriage. Having that answer, along with an amazing therapist helped me to cope. Having Spencer at my side the entire time helped even more. We'd both taken time off from work, Max stepping up and running both sides of things for a bit while we worked through everything, including our relationship with my father.

During this time, Spencer had also dealt with Brittany. She'd appeared at our home to pick Nikki up, a month after we'd lost the baby, and spewed some horrible, hateful words at me. Then she'd taken Nikki back home with her. Two days later, we'd gotten a call from Brittany's neighbour who had noticed she hadn't been home but knew Nikki had been staying there. She'd left Nikki unattended for two days. Immediately, Spencer called his lawyer, and they awarded us immediate custody. Then we had a restraining order placed against her.

Nikki danced around the living room wearing her little flower girl dress as Carly and I watched her, laughing at her silliness.

"Ainsley, what flowers am I getting?" she asked.

I smiled. "Well, I am not sure what they will have. It might look something like this," I said, turning my laptop around for her to see one image from another person's wedding. The flower girl was carrying hibiscus flowers.

"Oh, those are pretty. Can we plant those in the backyard?" she asked.

"I don't know if those will grow well here, sweetie," I said, kissing her forehead. "We need to get you out of this dress though."

"Oh, but it's soooo pretty," she said, doing another spin.

"Come on, Nikki, let's get you changed, and then we

can see Ainsley in her dress," Carly said, guiding her down the hall to her room.

I let out my breath, the flutters of nerves hitting my stomach. I looked at the bag that hung on the back of the walk-in closet door. I hadn't looked at this dress since I'd picked it up after the alterations had been done. I walked over and lowered the zipper. I looked at the beautiful dress I'd chosen almost six months ago and slipped the straps off the hanger. I worried about the weight I'd lost. It had been a struggle for a while to eat after I'd lost the baby. I had worked hard but I wasn't sure I'd gained enough back for the dress to fit any longer. I took off my shirt and my jeans and stepped into the dress and was surprised when it slid on like a glove. I reached behind me and raised the zipper as far as I could until I saw Carly standing in the door.

"Can you help me?"

"Wow, Ainsley, you look gorgeous," she said, coming over and raising the zipper the rest of the way. I turned around and looked at my friend, who, for the first time, had tears in her eyes because of something like this. "Spencer is going to bust when he sees you," she cried, straightening the lower part of the dress so that it hung straight.

"You think?" I smiled, looking at my reflection in the mirror.

"Wow, Ainsley, you are sooo pretty!" Nikki cried with excitement as she covered her mouth with her little hands.

"Isn't she though," Carly said, standing up and giving me another onceover.

We stood there for a moment, admiring my dress, when we heard a car door slam outside. I looked at Carly, my eyes bugging out of my head as panic filled me. "Is that Spencer?" I asked. I'd hidden the bag in the back of the closet, and we'd gone this long without him seeing it. I didn't want to ruin the surprise because he walked in after a long day at work to find me standing in it.

Carly ran over to the window and looked out, breathing a sigh of relief. "It's Jane." She giggled and ran down the hall to open the front door.

Moments later, Carly returned with Jane. One look at me and she smiled. "Goodness, Ainsley, you're breathtaking," she said, coming over and shoving my long hair off my shoulders.

"Thank you."

"Just wait until your father sees you in this dress. I think it might make him cry." She laughed.

I gave myself another look in the mirror and glanced at the clock. "Can you guys please help me out of this dress before Spencer gets here?"

"Of course," Carly said, coming behind me and unzipping the zipper, while Jane stood in front of me, taking the straps so the dress didn't fall to the floor. Together, they hung it back in the bag and zipped it up, slipping it behind the bag that held Spencer's suit while I got dressed.

"Everyone have their passports?" I questioned.

"Yes, your fathers just came in today," Jane said. "We were getting worried, but I got a notice from the post office. I just got it before I came here."

"I'm home," I heard Spencer call from the hallway. "Is it safe to come in?"

The three of us laughed. "Yes, of course," I called, throwing my T-shirt over my head.

Spencer rounded the corner, carrying a small bag and his laptop bag, and set them both in the corner. "Are we having a party?" he asked, looked from me to Carly to Jane.

"Just here, helping make sure everything is ready for tomorrow," Carly sang.

"And is it?" Spencer asked.

The three of us smiled, and I nodded my head. "Yes. Now, what is in that bag?" I questioned, curiosity getting the best of me.

"That," Spencer said, nodding to the bag, "is for our wedding night." He placed a kiss on my lips.

I felt my cheeks flush as Carly and Jane watched the exchange between us.

"Ohhh, what is it?" Nikki asked, running over to grab the bag, but Spencer grabbed it first, picking it up and placing it on the top of our dresser.

"It's not for a little person's eyes," Spencer said, grabbing her and throwing her over his shoulder. She let out a loud laugh as he tickled her before he placed her back down on the ground.

"I'm going to hit the shower and then get packed," Spencer said, heading to our ensuite shutting the door behind him.

Carly, Jane, Nikki, and I headed to the kitchen, where we sat down at the table to go over all the information for the trip. Spencer and I were to be married two days after we arrived, then we would be whisked away to a private part of the resort to spend our honeymoon, while the rest of the guests partied the week away.

"You're sure you'll be fine to watch Nikki?" I asked Carly.

"Of course. It's only for the wedding night, right?"

I nodded. "Yes."

"We can help too," Jane said. "We'd be happy to."

I smiled. "Thank you."

Things between my father and I, and Spencer and him, had changed in the days that followed the miscarriage. My father had been the rock that Spencer had needed, and he'd been there for me when I needed him as well. We'd had all the support we both needed, perhaps more. It was a welcome change, and soon Dad and Jane were visiting us more at the new place than they did when we lived next door.

"All right, who the hell is ready to party?" I asked, throwing my book to the side. I'd gone over and over all these plans for the last three months, to where there was really nothing left to plan.

"Yes!" Jane said, throwing her arms up in excitement.

Carly let out a laugh as she pulled Nikki close to her.

"I should get home. Your father will be home any minute, and I've got to get dinner ready and finish packing."

"Oh, me too," Carly said, jumping up out of her seat.

"Don't forget your dress," I said, running down the hall and grabbing her bridesmaid dress from the closet.

"I won't, don't worry. I also can't wait to meet Spencer's brother. You said he was single, right?" Carly asked, taking the dress from me.

I rolled my eyes and giggled. "Don't start."

Ainsley

Carly had just zipped up the back of my dress when a knock came to her door. Jane walked over, pulling it open. The wedding planner stood there holding a small pillow that contained our rings for Nikki to carry, along with my bouquet.

She came right in, handing Nikki the pillow and showing her how to hold it, then she came over to me and placed the bouquet in my hand. I smiled as I looked down at the tropical flowers.

"Okay, so we are heading to the beach," she said. "Nikki, you will walk beside me. Carly, you will be next, and Ainsley, of course, you will be last. We will meet your father down there, and that is when the ceremony will begin."

I swallowed hard and nodded, hoping that everything would go smoothly.

"What about Spencer, Max, and Mike?" I questioned.

She smiled. "They are already down there. I just left them before I came here."

I let out a breath as she took Nikki by the hand. "Ready?" she asked, looking down at her.

Nikki nodded her head, and we began the walk toward my future. People turned their heads and watched as we made our way through the resort. Carly walked beside me, holding the back of my dress up out of the sand.

"You ready?" she asked, leaning into me.

"Never been more ready for anything in my life," I said, smiling at her.

"I'm thrilled for you," she whispered.

"Thank you."

Things between us grew quiet for a moment. Then she leaned in. "Can I tell you something?"

"Of course."

"I wanted to apologize to you. I really was wrong about Spencer. He really is a good man. I am so happy that you found him."

I laughed. "Found him? Well, in all fairness, I practically stalked the man." I giggled, thinking back to when I'd set up that ridiculous profile through his website just to speak to the man I lived beside.

"I know. I just wanted you to know that I was wrong. I never really gave him a chance."

"It's okay," I said, stopping and wrapping my arms around my best friend. "You've always been overprotective, and I know now that you were just looking out for me."

"I was."

We continued on our way toward the wedding gazebo we had chosen down at the end of the beach, finally coming to the end of the path. I glanced through the trees and caught sight of Spencer standing beside his brothers, talking. He looked so handsome in his dark suit. As I watched him, I noticed little things. He fiddled with his watch, then the button on his suit jacket. Then he laughed again at something Mike said before returning to the watch. Was he nervous?

I smiled, and then I heard Carly let out a little gasp as she, too, looked in the same direction. "Are you okay?" I whispered while the wedding coordinator spoke to Jane.

"Hmmm, yes," Carly said, a light blush on her cheek.

I glanced through the trees and saw Max standing there looking toward us as he spoke to Spencer. Then I turned and looked at my best friend. She was watching his every move, her cheeks flushed.

I softly smiled to myself, then nudged Carly. "I know what, or should I say who, you are watching." I giggled. "Perhaps a little crush going on here?"

"Maybe." Carly giggled.

They'd hit it off last night and spent most of the evening sitting at the bar, talking. When Max offered to walk Carly back to her room, Spencer and I glanced at one another.

I was about to lean in and say something when I saw the men take their positions, and then the Bohemian music began playing, and Nikki headed toward the gazebo carrying the little pillow that contained our rings.

As the music played, I took my father's elbow, and we stood together while Nikki and Carly started toward the gazebo. My father turned to me and smiled. "You look gorgeous, Ainsley. Just like your mother did the day we wed," he whispered.

It was the first time I'd ever heard my father reference my mother as being beautiful, and a tear escaped my eyes. "Thanks, Daddy. I'm so glad you are here."

"Me too," he whispered, leaning in and kissing my cheek. "I feel like I lost a lot of time with you because it was so hard for me to come to grips to hand you over to this man, but I know in my heart this is the right thing for you. I'm sorry for all you've lost."

A tear slipped down my cheek. My father wiped it away with his rough fingers. "I can't walk you down the aisle in tears," he said, leaning in and kissing me on the cheek. "It's supposed to be the happiest day of your life."

"It is, Dad. I am happy." I sniffled.

When the wedding coordinator signaled to us, my father looked over at me as I let out a breath. "Ready?" he asked me quietly.

"Never been so ready in my life," I whispered back.

Together we took the first few steps, and when I looked up, my eyes locked with Spencer's. All the memories came flooding into my mind. The first time I saw him over the fence in his backyard, the first time he'd turned those blue eyes toward mine and allowed them to run the length of my body, the first time his hand brushed my cheek and his lips brushed mine.

A flood of emotion waved over me as his eyes trailed my body. When we approached, my father leaned in and whispered something to Spencer, and then placed my hand in his. I took a step closer to Spencer. He looked down into my face. "You look absolutely stunning," he whispered to me as he leaned in and placed a gentle kiss on my cheek.

A gentle breeze blew as the wedding official began speaking. We stood listening to the words he spoke, each of us taking them in. Then he looked at us both. "It's time for the vows."

I swallowed hard. Spencer and I had written our own vows, and while I'd run over my words with Carly a hundred times, butterflies still floated around my stomach as I worried I may forget them.

I looked at Spencer as he took both of my hands in his.

He looked at the ground and then up at me, looking me directly in the eyes.

"Ainsley, my love. It is with great pride I take you for my wife. We have proven to each other that together we can weather any storm that life presents."

I watched as he swallowed hard, his eyes looking a little glassy.

"In you, I have found my forever partner."

I blinked hard as my vision became blurry, and I reached up to dab under my eyes before I had tears and makeup streaming down my face.

"In a short time, you have become my lover, my companion, but most of all, my best friend. With you by my side, I know I will never be lonely again. I get to have you every day and night for the rest of eternity as my lover, my wife, and soulmate. You're my love and my light."

Spencer turned to Max and held his hand out. Max reached down and untied the ring from the small pillow that Nikki held and handed it to Spencer.

Spencer turned back to me and took my hand in his, sliding the ring partway onto my finger. "Ainsley, I give you this ring as a sign of my love, that it is forever, eternal and never-ending," he said, gently placing the ring on my finger.

I swallowed hard as I met his eyes. I took his hands in mine again, hoping that he couldn't feel them shaking.

"Spencer, I am so lucky to call you mine. You are

everything that I dreamed of, and all that I will ever need. I'm so madly in love with you, and I promise that my love for you will only grow stronger with each day that passes. I promise to be your friend and partner every step of the way, no matter what we may face."

Spencer's eyes were glued to mine as I swallowed hard, willing my voice not to shake.

"Today I give myself to you in marriage. To share my life in good times and bad. When our love is simple and when it's an effort, through whatever may cross our paths, I promise to cherish you and always hold you in the highest regard."

I turned to Carly, waiting while she removed the ring from the pillow and placed it in my hand.

I turned back to Spencer and met his eyes. "I vow to be here with you and for you today, and all the days of our lives. Spencer, I give you this ring as a sign of my love, that it is forever, eternal, and never-ending." I slipped the ring onto his finger and met his eyes. He smiled down at me as I smiled up at him.

"I would like to take this opportunity to present to everyone Mr. And Mrs. Spencer Brooks. You may now kiss your bride."

Spencer took a step closer to me and wrapped me in his arms, pulling me against him. He brought his hand to my cheek and met my lips, kissing me for the first time as my husband.

Ainsley

The room erupted with laughter as Carly said a few words at the end of dinner. She took her seat beside Max and whispered something to him.

Spencer had arranged for all of us to share a private dinner in one of the resort restaurants. We'd just finished eating and were waiting for dessert to be served. I slid my hand into his and met his eyes.

"I love you," he mouthed.

"I love you," I whispered.

"Who's up for dancing?" Carly questioned, looking around the table. "It's a wedding. Hell, we must dance."

"Oh, well, I think we are going to retire for the night after dinner," my father and Jane said in unison."

"Yeah, us too. It's been a long day," Mike and Trina replied.

"Spencer, Ainsley?" Carly questioned, looking at us, "It's your wedding, you guys have to dance!"

We both looked at one another and shook our heads. "Not tonight," Spencer answered.

"Jesus, it's their wedding night, for god sakes. I'm sure they have far more exciting things to do than go dancing," Max quipped, pushing into her with his shoulder.

"Also, aren't you supposed to be watching Nikki?" I questioned, looking at my best friend. "She needs to get to bed on time." I giggled, knowing full well it was already way past her bedtime.

Carly looked at me, smiling. "Yes, she can go with me."

"We will take Nikki for the night," Mike said. "Carly, you go dance."

"You sure? She is welcome with us as well," Jane answered, my father nodding his head.

I looked over to see Nikki let out a yawn and put her head down on the table, her eyes fighting to stay open.

"We'll stop by on our way back to the room and get her pajamas and clothes for the morning," Trina told me.

"Carly has them." I nodded in her direction.

Trina nodded, "Okay, I will get them from Carly."

"No problem, I'll get them from my room. Yet I still want to know, who is going to go dancing with me?" Carly pouted.

"Max?" Spencer said. "Do us a favor and take Carly dancing."

Max turned to Carly and grinned. "Sure thing, boss."

Dessert was served, and once we finished, Spencer grabbed my hand in his. "Everyone, I just want to thank you for joining us on our special day. Now, if you will excuse us, I am going to take my wife back to our room."

Spencer

Our suite was dimly lit as we made our way into the bedroom. I closed the door behind me and looked over at Ainsley. Her eyes reflected that same want and desire as mine. I walked over to her and allowed my fingers to graze over the skin on her arms, watching it pebble at my touch.

She closed her eyes as I reached behind her, slowly lowering the zipper on her dress. She raised her eyes to mine as I removed my suit jacket and shirt, then my pants. She leaned forward and placed a kiss on my chest as my fingers caught the shoulder straps of her dress. My fingers slid down the length of her arms, and the dress fell into a pile on the floor.

She stood before me in the white lace bra and thong

I'd gotten for her for today. "I've been waiting to get you out of that dress all day," I whispered as I bent and kissed her shoulder, then reached down and picked her up, carrying her over to the bed.

I placed her down on the bed, both of us moving toward the center. I leaned over to my side of the bed and opened the drawer, pulling out the surprise I'd gotten for Ainsley. I placed it beside my leg without her seeing it and then moved up and held my weight as I hovered over her. I placed a kiss on her chest and moved my way down, kissing the top of her breasts. I flicked the clasp open in front, her bra falling away.

Her nipples were already hard, begging me to take them in my mouth. I placed a kiss between her perfect tits as I allowed my hands to explore her body. I kissed my way down her body, running my tongue down her stomach, stopping at the start of her thong, allowing my fingers to play with the elastic.

I could feel my cock straining against my boxers. I opened her legs and once again held myself over her, allowing my cock to press between her legs with just enough pressure as I kissed her neck. I took one of her breasts in my hands, squeezing it, letting my hand play with it, and ran my thumb over the hardened nub.

"Take it in your mouth," Ainsley said quietly, arching her back.

I rolled her nipple between my thumb and forefinger,

and then sucked it into my mouth, grazing it with my teeth. A loud moan escaped her as I repeated that on the other side.

"I love these. So sensitive, so beautiful," I said, taking them both into my hands and rubbing my thumbs just under her nipples.

I kissed my way down her stomach, stopping at the elastic once again, and slipped them off her body. I forced her legs open, looking down at her slick, wet pussy. "So fucking wet," I hissed as I brought my lips to her center, lapping and sucking as I slid two fingers inside of her.

I listened to her moans as I continued, placing my hands under her ass so I could fuck her with my tongue. She moaned even louder when I continued flicking my tongue against her clit.

I could tell she was close, so I stopped and knelt before her, removing my boxers. I rested my one hand on the back of her thigh, angling her just right, while I gripped my cock with my free hand, giving it a couple pumps before I lined up with her entrance. One swift movement, and I was buried inside of my wife deeper than I'd ever been.

"Oh God, Spencer," she cried out as I thrust myself even deeper into her.

"What do you want?" I asked, gripping her waist.

"Make me come," she begged.

I repeated the short, deep thrust again, then reached

for the little finger vibrator I'd gotten. I slipped it onto my finger and placed one hand on the back of her thigh again, holding her in place. I hit the little switch, and a buzzing sound filled the room.

"What's that?" Ainsley questioned breathlessly.

"You'll see," I whispered, thrusting myself deeply into her before placing the little vibrator against her clit.

"Oh, fuck..." she screamed as I held that vibrator against her clit while I continued pumping into her.

"Let yourself go, baby," I said, reaching up and taking her nipple between my fingers and squeezing it.

I could feel her beginning to tighten as her body stiffened. I pulled the vibrator off her clit and began pumping into her hard and fast. "Spencer..." she screamed. I wrapped her in my arms and continued fucking my wife.

I felt her pussy clenching my cock as she came. I felt my balls tighten and allowed myself to let go, pouring myself into her.

Breathless and exhausted, I fell onto the mattress. I covered my eyes with my arm, my body covered in a sheen of sweat. I swallowed hard and let my body come down while Ainsley lay beside me, doing the same.

Ainsley

I lay there listening to him breathe. He'd been quiet now for twenty minutes, sometimes even lightly snoring. My eyes travelled over his muscular frame. Even though he'd just given me one of the best orgasms he'd ever given me, I wanted him again. I was ready.

I nuzzled into his neck, pressing my lips to his warm skin. "You awake?" I whispered.

"Barely," he muttered. "That was so fucking hot."

"Yes, it was," I said, leaning down and kissing his chest. When he didn't move, I looked down to his cock. My fingers trailed down his abs and over his hips, his cock beginning to stir at my touch. I looked back at him. His eyes were still closed.

I took a moment and took his cock in my hand, then I slid down, bringing his cock to my lips. I licked his shaft, running my tongue all the way up, letting my tongue hit the rim of the head before taking his cock all the way into my mouth.

He let out a deep breath as his fingers slipped into my hair. "That's it, baby," he said, his voice throaty. "Fuck, suck me."

I took him all the way to the back of my throat, my hand working him, the other cupping his balls. The more I sucked, the harder he fisted my hair. I pulled my mouth from him, running my tongue once again from the base of his cock all the way to the tip, in time to lick the drop of pre-cum that was waiting for me.

I crawled up his body and straddled his hips, reaching between my legs, grabbing his cock and lining him up with me. I slid down onto his cock, taking him in. I loved hearing the guttural groan that escaped him as I lifted myself up and slid back down.

His powerful hands gripped my hips, and he took control, guiding my movements as his eyes washed over my breasts. I loved how he watched me, how his eyes skimmed my naked body. He sat up, still working my hips. He sucked my nipple into his mouth, letting his teeth gently graze over it.

I could feel a flood of heat between my legs as he moved to the other one and repeated that again before he laid back. He adjusted the pillow behind his head so he could watch me as I rode him.

"That's it, baby. Ride my cock."

He reached for that little finger vibrator again, and I felt my excitement build as I watched him slip it onto his finger. He pushed me back, raising his knees up behind me for something to lean on so he could place it once again on my clit.

This time he'd turned the vibration up higher, and the second it touched me, I tightened around him. "God, Spencer, I can't."

"You can," he said, as he pulled it away for a moment,

then placed it against me again for only a second before removing it again.

"Please, Spencer..." I cried.

"Please what? Please do it again?" he asked, placing it against my clit for only a brief second.

I could feel my orgasm building each time he did that, and it faded as soon as he pulled it away.

He allowed me to stay on him for only a couple seconds more before he lifted me off his cock and flipped me around so I was on my knees. He pulled me back and slid himself into me from behind, fucking me hard.

"Yes..." I cried as he slammed into me. He reached around, placing that little vibrator on my clit while he continued at an unrelenting pace. I pulled at his hand, begging him to remove that little vibrator, but it was useless. He refused. He held himself deep inside of me as I felt an earth-shattering orgasm rip through my body, while Spencer emptied himself into me again.

Ainsley

Two months Later

"Hey, you meeting me for lunch or what?" Carly's voice erupted over the phone.

I smoothed down the sides of my skirt and fixed my shirt, turning to look over at Spencer, who stood with his pants down around his ankles, his shirt on the back of his office chair. We still hadn't seemed to pass through the honeymoon stage yet.

"I forgot about lunch," I mouthed to him. A smile came to Spencer's face as he reached around and rubbed my swollen clit, torturing me.

"Yep, Carly, sorry. I got, um... sidetracked. I'll be there in ten minutes," I said, closing my eyes as the feeling of release built inside of me again.

"Why are you out of breath, anyway?" she questioned. I heard her breath hitch. "Oh my God, you're not."

"No, I um... I ran to my desk from the washroom. I was expecting a call from a client."

"Uh-huh," she said.

"Look, I'll be there shortly."

"Hurry," Carly sang.

I put the receiver down on the cradle and turned to look at Spencer, who stood there with a smug look on his face.

"What?" he said, licking my arousal off his fingers.

"Nothing," I said, feeling completely frustrated again.

"Hey, I told you not to answer that." He chuckled.

"Well, I wasn't supposed to forget lunch. You distracted me again."

"Is that so?" Spencer said, coming over to me, running his hands over my bare arms. "Give me another five and I'll do it all over again," he whispered, biting my ear.

"No deal. I've got to go." I giggled then climbed up on my toes and pressed a kiss to his lips. "I'll see you at home?"

"Sorry I'm late!" I cried as I rushed over to the table where Carly sat.

"Jesus, it's about time. It's not like we have tomorrow, you know." Carly laughed.

Carly was headed to Denver. She'd been hired at a school there and was starting in two weeks. I'd gone with her to find a place and to help get her settled, and tomorrow she started on her new adventure.

"So, did you call Max and tell him you'd be in town starting tomorrow? I mean, he said to call once you got there," I questioned.

When Carly and I had gone to Denver, Spencer had arranged for us to stay at Max's apartment. Max had been more than welcoming, taking the day off to show us around the city, and then he'd told Carly that there was no reason they couldn't hang out together until she got settled and met some people. I knew he was probably only doing it because Spencer had told him to; nevertheless, I thought it was nice.

"Yeah, we've been messaging back and forth. He said he'd meet me at the airport if I wanted."

"Awesome."

We took a couple of minutes to order, and then I slid the bag I was carrying into my purse.

"What's that?" Carly questioned, looking at the rolled-up bag.

I had told no one, not even Spencer, but the last few mornings I'd woken up I'd not been feeling so hot. This morning had been the worst, and I'd thrown up right after Spencer left for work.

"It's nothing," I muttered.

Carly gave the same look she always gave when she knew I was hiding something. "Ainsley?"

I let out a breath. I'd been dying to tell someone. "Okay fine," I said, looking around the restaurant as if I were guarding a state secret. "Say nothing, but I bought a pregnancy test."

Carly's eyes lit up. "Oh goodness, really. You think you're pregnant?"

"Shhhh..." I said, bringing my forefinger to my lips. "Yes."

"Oh God, I hope so," she said, rubbing her hands together in excitement. "You better tell me what the answer is as soon as you know."

Spencer, Nikki, and I had just returned home after driving Carly to the airport. It was late, and Nikki was sound asleep in the back seat. Spencer carried her in, and we put her to bed.

"What do you say we take a bottle of wine and hit the hot tub?"

I paused. "That sounds great. I'm just going to head down to the bedroom and get changed. I'll meet you out there?"

"Sure, I'll get the wine and towels."

I wandered down the hall to the bedroom and pulled the bag containing the pregnancy test from my dresser drawer. Carrying it into the bathroom, I locked the door behind me. My stomach fluttered as I stared down at the box. I'd just picked it up to open it when Spencer knocked on the door.

"Ainsley, I need my robe."

"One minute." I shoved the box under the sink and took a breath, calming my nerves before opening the door and handing him his robe.

He smiled, then kissed me.

"I'll be right there."

"Take your time," he said, wrapping the robe around his already naked body.

I waited for him to leave the room and listened hard until I heard no noise before opening the cupboard door.

Staring down at the box for a few more seconds I decided to open it and remove one of the tests. "Moment of truth," I whispered to myself.

A few minutes later, I stared down at a positive result, my heart beating wildly in my chest. Excitement built inside of me as I wrapped the test in some paper and threw it into the garbage. I slipped out of my clothes and wrapped my robe around me, then slipped my feet into my slippers.

I wandered down the hall, stopping outside of the bedroom that was going to be our nursery. For the first time since the miscarriage, I opened the door and stepped inside. Spencer had the room painted as a surprise before we'd moved in, and he'd put together the crib together, which sat against the wall. That was as far as we'd gotten, and now, the room was empty. I walked over and ran my fingers over the edge of the crib, looking down, thinking of what could have been.

A tear slid down my cheek as I stood there. I wiped it away and took a deep breath. "Even though we never got to hold you, I loved you more than you'll ever know," I whispered to the empty room. "You'll be here forever in my hearts and thoughts."

I took a deep breath, turned, and made my way to the door. I looked back over my shoulder before I pulled it closed behind me and took a moment, wiping the tears from my eyes. I made my way to the back door and saw

Spencer already sitting in the hot tub, a glass of wine in his hand. I went to the cupboard and grabbed some water first, and then joined him. Setting my glass on the edge of the tub, I crawled in.

"Water? I was sure you were going to want some wine. I figured it would help calm you down after that crazy display of tears you and Carly shared tonight."

I laughed, thinking about how we had clung to one another in the airport as if we'd never see one another again. "I will, in time," I said, sliding over and placing myself on his lap.

"I think Carly was on to us this afternoon," I said, laughing. "She kept giving me a knowing look."

"Oh, I am sure she was."

"I mean, there is only one reason someone would sound as breathless as you did. Actually, thinking about it is turning me on." He chuckled, reaching under the water and pulling me into him.

"You sure it's not because you have a naked woman in your lap?"

"That could have a bit to do with it." He chuckled, meeting my lips. "What took so long? Everything okay?"

It took me a moment, but I nodded my head as I thought about how to tell him.

"You sure?" he questioned, worry creeping into his eyes.

I smiled. "Everything is perfect, Daddy," I whispered, kissing his lips.

When I pulled away, I first saw a look of confusion and then a glimpse of understanding in Spencer's eyes. "Seriously?" he questioned.

"Yes. Yes. Yes. Yes..." I cried, growing happier by the minute. "We are going to have a baby."

Spencer looked at me, tears in his eyes. "You okay?" he asked, holding me tight. "I mean, are you okay with this?"

I nodded, another small wave of sadness coming over me. "I'm going to be okay. It is going to take me some time again, but I couldn't be more excited."

He pressed his lips to mine. "Please tell me one thing."

"What's that?"

"Please tell me I know before Carly."

I giggled. "Yes, that was what took me so long."

"Thank God," he said, pulling me in again for another kiss. "I can't wait to make lots of babies with you," he said against my lips.

Spencer grew quiet, then cupped my cheek with his hand and slowly brought his lips to mine, his tongue washing through my mouth. What started out as what most people would call infatuation had turned out to be the best move I'd ever made.

Spencer Brooks was the most attractive man I'd ever laid eyes on... my father's best friend... the man I babysat for... and now, my husband.

Want more of Spencer and Ainsley?
GRAB THE BONUS SCENE

To get your FREE bonus scene visit
https://geni.us/SpencerBrooksBonus

What is coming next from S.L. Sterling

Willow Valley
Letters from the Heart
Preorder Here

Willow Valley
My Darling Christmas
Preorder Here

About the Author

USA Today Bestselling Author S.L. Sterling was born and raised in southern Ontario. She now lives in Northern Ontario Canada and is married to her best friend and soul mate and their two dogs.

An avid reader all her life, S.L. Sterling dreamt of becoming an author. She decided to give writing a try after one of her favorite authors launched a course on how to write your novel. This course gave her the push she needed to put pen to paper and her debut novel "It Was Always You" was born.

When S.L. Sterling isn't writing or plotting her next novel she can be found curled up with a cup of coffee, blanket and the newest romance novel from one of her favorite authors.

In her spare time, she enjoys camping, hiking, sunny destinations, spending quality time with family and friends and of course reading.

Catch up with me on social media!
Join my Reader Group

Sterlings Silver Sapphires

No social media? No problem, stay up to date with my Newsletter

Visit my Website

Other Titles by S.L. Sterling

It Was Always You

On A Silent Night

Bad Company

Back to You this Christmas

Fireside Love

Holiday Wishes

Saviour Boy

The Boy Under the Gazebo

The Greatest Gift

Into the Sunset

The Spencer Brooks Diaries

Our Little Secret

Our Little Surprise

Our Little Wedding

The Malone Brother Series

A Kiss Beneath the Stars

In Your Arms

His to Hold

Finding Forever with You

Vegas MMA

Dagger

Doctors of Eastport General

Doctor Desire

Doctor Right

All I Want for Christmas (Contemporary Romance Holiday
Collection)

Constraint (KB Worlds: Everyday Heroes)

Willow Valley

Memories of the Past

The Holiday Dilemma

* 9 7 8 1 9 8 9 5 6 6 6 5 7 *